5

The Devil's

By Paul Evan

POWERFUL NEW BOOK-LENGTH NOVEL, Complete In This Issue

*The set-up in Calder town was a familiar one to Bill Borden,
but each helltown has its own individual mysteries. And what
Borden couldn't figure out was how a man like Monk Malone,
who was apparently the boss of Calder, could operate in such a
stupid manner. For, although the organization Malone rodded
was intricate and clever, Monk himself didn't seem to show much
savvy. Or was his apparent dumbness a trap for Borden?*

3

COMPLETE
COWBOY
NOVEL
Magazine

Volume 8, Number 4

April, 1949

COMPLETE COWBOY NOVEL MAGAZINE published bi-monthly by COLUMBIA PUBLICATIONS, INC., 1 Appleton Street, Holyoke, Mass., Editorial and executive offices at 241 Church St., New York 13, New York. Entered as second class matter at the Post Office at Holyoke, Mass. Single copy 15c. yearly subscriptions 90c. Entire contents copyrighted 1949 by Columbia Publications, Inc. Manuscripts must be accompanied by self-addressed stamped envelopes to insure return if not accepted, and while reasonable care will be exercised in handling them, they are submitted at author's risk. Printed in the U. S. A.

ROBERT W. LOWNDES, Editor

Doorstep

Lehman

Borden tackled the fleeing drygulcher while the townspeople watched.

1

Rough And Tough

IT WAS noon when Bill Borden rode into Calder and just about five seconds after noon when he realized that the fuse to some sort of explosion had been lighted and was sizzling.

To begin with: while the street was crowded there wasn't a single horse or vehicle at the hitching rails; secondly; the people seemed to be milling about rather than heading for any definite destination; and finally, their very expressions were those of expectation. There were murmurs but no noise, and Bill heard no joking or laughter; that meant that whatever was about to happen would be grim.

The street stretched dusty and empty before him; he would feel like a one man parade riding along it. So he didn't ride along it; he cut back into the alley, rode along it to the center of the town, then up another passageway between the *Frontier* saloon and a barber shop, and reined in at the sidewalk. He shifted his weight in the saddle and rolled a cigarette, letting his gaze roam over the crowd on the far side of the street as he did so.

One figure caught his attention immediately. It was that of a tall, raw-boned man with a mane of gray hair brushed straight back from a high forehead and hanging almost to his shoulders. His bony face was smooth-shaven and deeply lined, and the dark eyes beneath bushy brows burned with the fire of the zealot. He wore black trousers and a black cutaway coat. A gambler? No, thought Bill; those gnarled hands clenched into fists at his side denoted power rather than skill.

A girl stood beside him, her hand clutching his arm. She was blonde and pretty, and beside him she appeared very tiny. Her blue eyes were large and frightened. She could be his daughter, judged Bill.

His gaze traveled on and came to rest on another woman. He cataloged her quickly; young, dark, neat and pretty. Her expression was grim but not scared. Both girls appeared out of place in this rough, raw town. He had heard Calder referred to as Hell's

Back Yard and The Devil's Doorstep; these young women were better suited to stand at the gateway to Heaven, so far as looks went.

Besides these three, Bill saw only what he had expected to see in a town which was the haven for fugitives from the law. There were a few men who appeared to be tradesmen and a few women who might have been their wives or daughters; these were component parts of any Western frontier town. For the rest, there were a number of flannel-shirted miners, a sprinkling of tinhorn gamblers, a great many coarse-featured, roughly dressed, well-heeled roughs, and a dozen or so slatterly women with the stamp of the honky-tonk upon them. These latter were not scared either; they were excited and avidly curious.

A stir like that which galvanizes a crowd at the approach of the circus parade swept through the spectators. Men stopped moving about, and heads were turned to gaze up the street. An almost inaudible whisper of "Here he comes!" ran along the sidewalk; then, like an undulating wave, the ranks surged backwards to crowd against the buildings and into doorways until but three persons remained where they had originally stood—on the far side of the street. They were the tall, rawboned man; the blonde girl beside him; and the young, dark and pretty one.

So it was to be a shooting affair! Bill leaned forward in his saddle and gazed in the direction the others were looking.

A MAN WAS coming down the middle of the street. He was not big, but there was confidence and fixety of purpose in his stride. He was dressed like a dude, with an enormous cream-colored Stetson hat, an ornate calfskin vest, whipcord trousers and black Spanish-leather boots. His cartridge belt was hand-tooled and studded with gold, the holster slung low and tied down, and the butt plates of his Colt were of mother-of-pearl. Bill's nose wrinkled; this was a professional gunman *de luxe.*

As though jerked by a hidden wire, all heads turned to gaze in the opposite direction, and Bill, too, followed the tug of the string. Another man had stepped into the street at the end recently traversed by Bill.

He was big, ruddy-faced, with a huge mustache and calm, blue eyes. He shuffled along the street pushing the dust away with his boots. He wore the plain, serviceable garb of a cowman; his cartridge belt and holster were black and slick from use and his .44 had a plain walnut butt. This man, decided Bill, was a fighter but not a killer, with a confidence born of knowledge that his cause was a just one—rather than the assurance that his draw was fast and his aim sure.

And now, from the doorway of a saloon on the other side, emerged half a dozen cowboys, keen-eyed and poker faced. They moved along the plank sidewalk slightly behind the big man, treading warily, spacing themselves so as not to get in each other's way. The big man turned his head and made an annoyed gesture but they paid no attention; whether he liked it, they were going to see that he got a square deal. When he was fifty feet away, Bill turned his head and glanced again at the professional gunman; he was about the same distance to Bill's right. Borden couldn't have picked a better place had he known in advance what was going to happen.

Both men advanced steadily. The spectators w e r e silent, pressing against the walls or crowded into doorways. Bill could see the faces of the more timid behind windowpanes.

The men were eighty feet apart— seventy—sixty.

They slowed their pace slightly, becoming careful, wary. The dark-haired young woman stood at the edge of the street, every muscle tense, every nerve taut, her eyes fixed on the big man as though, by some mental process, she could add her strength and courage to that of his own. The big rawboned one directly opposite Bill was gazing steadily at the approaching gunman as though to halt him by the very intensity of that gaze; the blonde girl was gripping his arm with both hands now.

Fifty feet apart. Within the next ten feet—

The tall, rawboned man across the street lifted a bony hand and gently removed the girl's fingers from his arm. He pushed her back with a long arm, then stepped out into the middle of the street, halting between the two men, facing the smaller one. He raised his right hand, palm outward; both men took a stride or two more, then came to a halt.

The rawboned man spoke in a deep, impressive voice. *"Thou shalt not kill!* It's the Lord's commandment; it must be obeyed." ·

A parson! thought Bill. *A parson in Calder!.*

The gunman spoke without moving his lips. "Get outa the way!"

"You and all the evil in you cannot move me, Smoke Rafferty." The parson said it quietly, but his voice grew in volume as he continued. "The gold which the evil forces of this town would pay you for the murder of John Turner will not be earned. I am the Lord's representative here in Calder and I say you shall not kill him."

A shout came from somebody in the crowd. "Stand aside, Parson, and see whose side the Lord's on!"

The preacher did not remove his intent gaze from the face of Smoke Rafferty. He said, "Blasphemy is one of the lesser sins of this evil town; we will concern ourselves with the greater ones first."

Rafferty sidestepped, his hand flashing his gun, but the parson sidestepped with him. The gun came up to cover him, but he did not falter.

Rafferty swore. "Get outa the way or I'll let you have it!"

On the sidewalk, six guns cleared as many holsters; one of the cowboys called, "You do, Smoke, and we'll blast you out of yore fancy boots!"

BILL BORDEN watched with narrowed eyes, his gaze moving swiftly from one actor to another in this drama. The cowman, John Turner, had halted twenty feet behind the parson; he stood with legs slightly spread, his body bent, and his right arm crooked. An equal distance in front of the preacher stood Smoke Rafferty, his face no longer imperturbable but white with anger; he had lowered the muzzle of his gun under the threat of cowboy Colts.

Bill glanced again at the big preacher standing like a monolith between the two men; then his attention was caught by a flutter of white from the sidewalk. Above the preacher's head he saw a raised arm and a hand with a white handkerchief. It waved once and then was lowered.

A shot boomed out.

Bill jerked his head to the right and upward; the shot had come from above him. He heard a startled cry and looked back at John Turner again. The man was teetering on his heels; he had dropped the gun he had instinctively drawn and both hands were pressed against his chest. The calm blue eyes were wide, his lower jaw sagged as though with consternation; he took a staggering step then plunged face-down in the dust.

There was an instant of horrified silence in which every movement was arrested; then savage cries broke out and people flooded into the street from both sides. The cowboys raised their sixguns and blasted away at the flat roof of the *Frontier;* the air stirred to the rush of leaden slugs that thudded into the false front or whined away into space.

Bill wheeled his horse and spurred him down the forty-foot passage to the alley. As he turned into it he saw a horse standing at the far corner of the saloon; above it, suspended by hands which clung to the eaves, was a man. The man let go and dropped into saddle, the horse bounding away the instant he hit leather.

Bill was close and his pony was running all out, now. Two great bounds took him to the rump of the other's horse. The man flung a startled glance over his shoulder, then whipped out his gun and twisted in the saddle. Bill slipped his right foot from the stirrup, put his weight on the left, and flung himself at the fellow as though about to wrestle down a steer.

His left hand went about the six-gun, the forefinger wedging itself between chamber and firing pin of the drawn hammer; the other arm went about the fellow's waist. Gravity and momentum did the rest; the horses kept going, but Bill's weight dragged the man from his saddle and they landed in the dust of the alley.

Bill still clung to the gun; he couldn't have let go had he wanted to, for the hammer, released, had driven its sharp firing pin deep into the flesh of his forefinger. He wrenched and the gun came free, still clinging to his hand. He was beneath the other, but a quick roll reversed their positions; Borden held himself tightly clamped to the other, his face pressed against the man's chest, and the blows which the other struck landed feebly on his back.

SIX COWBOYS came surging around the corner of the Frontier and let out shouts of vengeance at sight of the two on the ground. Rough hands tore them apart and dragged them to their feet.

"Which one of you was it?" asked their leader grimly.

Bill nodded towards the other. "Caught him as he was dropping off the roof; nailed him when he hit the saddle."

One of the cowboys said, "That's straight goods, Wes. I seen this pilgrim settin' his hoss when John was shot, seen him rein around and head back here. If it hadn't been for him this lousy killer would'a got clean away."

They released Bill immediately and turned their attention to the killer. "Take him down to the livery corral. String him up over the gate."

They yanked him away, as he protested wildly.

People came streaming back into the alley, one of them a paunchy individual with a scraggly mustache and pop eyes. He had a nickeled star on his vest, and he blustered, "Hey! What you fellers aimin' to do? I'll take charge of the prisoner."

They told him profanely where he could go, and he followed them down the alley, arguing heatedly to deaf ears that he was the law and would handle the situation.

Bill drew the firing pin out of his forefinger, tossed the gun aside, then tore off a bit of cigarette paper and wet it, stuck it over the wound to stop the bleeding. His horse was standing a short distance away; Bill got on him and rode around the Frontier to the street. The whole town was humming. They had carried John Turner's body into the store and there was a crowd on the steps and the sidewalk outside. Bill dismounted, tied in front of the Frontier and went inside.

There was excitement here, too, although it was subdued. The bartender who poured Borden's drink was nervous and jerky in his movements; the hard-looking men along the bar were tight-lipped and for the most part silent. Their very silence was eloquent, and their eyes glinted with something akin to satisfaction; clearly they belonged to the "evil forces" that, for some reason, had wanted to see John Turner killed.

The doors swung inward and Calder's marshal pushed between them, his face red and his pop eyes standing out on stems. He stamped angrily past the bar, saying, "Monk inside?" The bartender nodded and the marshal cut around the end of the bar, rapped on a door, opened it and went in. As the door was opened, Bill caught a glimpse of a big, hard-faced man behind a desk with a glass in his hand; it was a mean face with a broad, squat nose, thick lips and heavy jowls.

Almost immediately the marshal came out. He closed the door and raised his voice. "Turner's men are takin' Sam Sneed to the livery corral to hang him; I aim to stop 'em. Any of you fellers that want to come along, raise yore right hands and take the deputy's oath."

A dozen hands went up; the hands of everybody in the place except himself and the two bartenders, Bill noticed. The marshal mumbled some words and said in the same breath, "Come along." He marched out to the street with them crowding after him.

Bill said to the bartender, "Mighty

efficient marshal you got; raises a posse in no time."

The bartender poured himself a shot and downed it. "Yeah, Biff's a good man."

"Biff?"

"Name's Bang. Cliff Bang. Folks call him Biff."

"Biff Bang, huh? Catchy name for a lawman. Wonder why he didn't try to stop that shooting between Rafferty and Turner."

"Why should he? That was a personal affair. Smoke and John had it and Smoke told John to stay on the range where he belonged or come prepared to shoot his way into town; Turner come."

"Hm-m. Biff Bang always come running to Monk—whoever he is— when he wants to raise a posse?"

"Sure. Monk Malone's the mayor of Calder."

The man was observing Bill intently. He said, "Stranger, ain't you?"

"That's right; heard of your nice little town and thought I'd like to look it over."

The barman got a rag and started to mop the bar. "Nice town, all right. Stands on its own feet; don't put up with no interference by Rangers and such-like. If you got any troubles, pilgrim, just take 'em to Monk Malone; he'll see you through."

Bill went outside. He was at the hitching rail untying the rein when a girl's voice said, "Excuse me; I've been looking all over for you."

The Lowdown

 ILL turned and saw the young, dark, pretty girl. The top of her dusky head came just about to his chin, and a close view showed her to be even neater than he had first thought her.

She said, "I saw you turn your horse and go back to the alley just after John Turner was shot. You must be the one who caught Sam Sneed as he came off the roof; what's your name?"

"Kriss Kringle," he told her solemnly. "But you can call me Kriss."

"You're a bit reticent, aren't you?"

"Does that mean I forgot my whiskers?"

"It means that you're backward about giving your real name. I'm used to that in Calder; we have so many faces without names. But you did nab Sam Sneed, didn't you?"

"It was nothing," he said modestly. "He emptied his sixgun and two double-barreled shotguns loaded with buckshot at me; but I just took off my hat, brushed the bullets aside, dived twenty feet and caught him by an ankle, waved him around my head and—"

"Just a minute! You fibbed to me. You told me you were Kriss Kringle; you're not. You're Paul Bunyon. But before we get any farther into this I'd better explain."

"I think you'd better."

"I'm Molly Sexton. My father owns and publishes the Calder *Clarion* and I'm his star—and only—reporter. My curiosity is entirely professional, Mr. Kringle. Or is it Bunyon?"

He grinned. "Bill Borden. Bill to the press."

"Thanks, Bill. Now tell me all about it, won't you? You see, it's important; John Turner was the Cleanup Party's candidate for mayor, and his murder has a political significance."

He considered her gravely. She was no longer smiling; there was pain and something akin to despair in her fine dark eyes.

"Tell you what; I'll give you the story in exchange for the lowdown on Calder; I'm interested. I've heard it called "Murderers' Hole and "The Devil's Doorstep" and "Hell's Back Yard," and I want to know—"

Molly didn't learn just then what it was he wanted to know, for from some distance down the street came a sudden shouting and the sound of scattered gunfire. She turned and took three steps in that direction, then stopped. "Darn it! I'm a lady and not suppposed to run. What is it, Bill?"

"Want to find out?" asked Bill and ducked under the hitching rail. He stepped into the saddle, reined over beside the sidewalk and kicked his right f o o t free of the stirrup. "Hop on and I'll hold you."

She hesitated, flushing, and he grinned down at her a bit sardonically. "Is the fearless reporter scared?"

She tossed her dark curls and returned his look defiantly. "For the sake of the press," she said, and gripped his extended arm with both hands.

He raised her off the ground and when her foot found the stirrup, quickly put his arm about her waist. "Hang on," he said, and touched the pony with steel.

It is possible that he thought to scare her; it is even possible that he expected her to cling desperately to him. She didn't scare and she didn't cling; her eyes were bright and her dark hair whipped back in the breeze, but she rode relaxed in the circle of his arm, her chin held high and her lips set.

It wasn't much of a ride; a hundred yards or so down the street and Bill swerved into a passageway beside the livery stable. They swung around a corner into the alley and were on the scene of the battle. Wes and his five cowboys were withdrawing along the alley presenting an unbroken front which bristled with sixguns. The marshal's posse had taken to cover; Bill could see them crouching behind barrels and wagons and standing in doorways. When one showed part of his anatomy there was a blast of sixgun fire to persuade him that discretion was the better part of valor. Over at the corral, a man sat with his back to a post; he was nursing a broken arm and swearing monotonously.

Bill said, "We'd better get out of here or we'll be holding up a post ourselves," and reined quickly back into the passageway. Molly Sexton had stiffened and when he glanced at her he saw that her face was chalk white.

He said, "Is our star reporter scared?"

"Our star reporter is slightly ill. Bill, did you see it?"

Bill had; he'd turned back into the passageway in hope that she wouldn't. "It was dangling from a rope tied to the crossbar over the corral gate, and it was still swinging and twisting gently."

"Sure, I saw it. Don't you think I'd better deliver you at your office so you can write the story?"

"You can deliver me at the office, period. I won't be able to write until I stop shaking, and I think it would be better if you put me down where I have something solid under me."

Bill lowered her to the ground, then dismounted and walked beside her, leading his horse. They turned the corner into the street, walked half a block, then halted before a one-story frame building with the words CALDER CLARION painted on the big window. Bill tied his horse at a hitching post and followed Molly Sexton into the building.

THERE WAS but one big room, and the front third of this was divided from the rest by a wooden railing. On Bill's side of the railing were two battered desks, several straightbacked chairs, a safe, and a cupboard which served as a filing cabinet. Beyond the railing were a Washington hand press, a job press, a compositor's bench holding type, and the various bits of equipment and odds and ends necessary in the printing business.

Molly sat down at one of the desks and waved Bill to a chair. He drew it up and she found a pad of paper and a pencil. "Now," she said, "the whole thing, and don't spare your modesty."

He told her briefly of Sam Sneed's capture.

"When you write it up, just forget the name Bill Borden. Make it Kriss Kringle or Paul Bunyon or little Lord Fauntleroy, but don't mention Bill Borden."

She raised her eyebrows at him. "Nobody will offer to pin a medal on you, if that's what bothers you."

"I wouldn't mind that. What I'm afraid of is that somebody might want to erect a monument to my memory—first making sure that I am a memory."

"Afraid!" she taunted. "The valiant hero who seized the villain by a leg and waved him around in the air!"

"Scared to death," he admitted, much too readily. He grinned, then sobered. "No fooling, Molly; keep the Borden part out of it; I told you my name in a moment of weakness and now I'm asking you to forget it, pronto."

She said, "Oh!" and her face clouded. "I suppose I understand. Just another face without a name. Well, I'll keep your dark secret locked in my breast as a privileged communication. Bill, if you're hiding from the law you'd better keep moving; you're safe enough now, but after election it's going to be different. Calder has sunk deep enough in the mud; we're going to drag it out and air it."

"We?" It was Bill's eyebrows that went up now.

"We. I don't care how bad a town is, there are always folk who want to be able to look people in the face when they say where they're from. They're long suffering and patient, but the time finally comes when they rise up in their wrath and drive the money lenders from the Temple. There are dozens of examples—Abilene, Tombstone, Hangtown and others like them. In time they were cleaned up; and it was the decent people who cleaned them, just as the decent people of Calder are going to clean up this town."

"It'll take a lot of cleaning. How do you aim to go about it?"

"By persuasion if possible; by force if necessary. The first Tuesday of next month is election day. The people choose a mayor and three councilmen; the mayor and councilmen change from time to time but only as Malone elects. They play ball with him or else. The marshal is his man and won't even take a chew of tobacco without asking his permission."

Bill sat with outthrust feet and with thumbs hooked in his cartridge belt, looking at her from under the brim of his hat. She regarded him steadily. "A man hiding from the law makes his arrangements with Malone. Although it might be hard to get proof, we're pretty certain that Monk takes care of the wanted for a certain monetary consideration. The amount charged probably depends upon the enormity of the crime."

She pressed her lips tightly together, then opened them suddenly and said, "Bill, what are you running from? What did you do?"

Bill looked startled. "Me?"

"Yes, you. I want to know. What crime did you commit?"

"Gosh! Do I have to tell?"

"I wish you would. I'm hoping it wasn't too awful."

Bill sagged in his chair and lowered his head. "It was terrible," he said in a low, shamed voice. He looked up at her with misery in his eyes. "I set fire to an orphan asylum just to hear the kids squeal."

"Bill!" Her eyes were angry and her cheeks pink. "All right; don't tell me. Whatever it was I hope they catch you and give you a good long term in the penitentiary." She fiddled with the papers on her desk while he sat there grinning at her. She said, "Well, you asked for the lowdown on Calder and now you have it. Father's a crusader and loves to fight for the right; he moved in and started the Clarion, and I help him. Reverend Ernest Rutherford came to preach the Gospel; he holds services in a tent at the end of town. His daughter Nancy plays the melodion and leads the singing."

Bill said, "You'll have a hard time persuading these roughs to vote the Cleanup ticket by tossing editorials and hymns at them. The only talk they savvy is gun talk, and the way to persuade 'em is with a club."

"We hope to outvote them. The cattlemen are with us; they're sick and tired of having their men come to town to be robbed, beaten and thrown into jail. The cowboys will vote the way their bosses vote; it's a matter of loyalty with them."

"How about the tradespeople and the miners?"

"We're working on them. The tradespeople are scared of Monk Malone; the miners rarely vote. They seldom stay in one place long enough to be interested; they hear of a new strike and away they go. Reverend Rutherford is working on them; he visits their camps frequently with Nancy. The miners adore her, and I don't blame them; she's the nearest thing to an angel that you can find on this earth."

"I've always wanted to meet an angel," said Bill dreamily.

MOLLY Sexton looked searchingly at Bill, but before she could speak the door opened and two men came in. One was a rugged, carelessly-dressed man in his forties; the other was not much older than Borden. He was well built, brown and handsome, with dark hair and mustache and flashing blue eyes. He was dressed conservatively but neatly.

The elder man spoke quickly. "Molly, have you this awful affair written up? We have to get out an extra at once. John Turner died a martyr's death and the good element is shocked and angry. I don't know what we'll do without him, but one thing is certain; his murder will swing many a doubtful vote our way. I wish we could come out flatly and accuse Malone, but we haven't a shred of proof. Sam Sneed died without telling who had hired him to kill John.".

"I've covered it pretty well," said Molly. "Dad, I want you to meet—this gentleman. He's the one who caught Sam, and he's given us the story. Bill, this is my father, Leander Sexton."

Sexton gripped Bill's hand. "I'm glad to know you, Bill. That was quick work on your part; if you hadn't acted so promptly we'd never have known who shot John." He turned to the other man. "This is Fred Sivart; he is one of the staunchest supporters of the reform movement."

Sivart flashed Bill a quick smile and shook his hand, "We certainly can use some reform in Calder," he said.

"Fred owns the *Double Eagle* saloon and gambling hall," explained Sexton. "He's a bit self-conscious because of his profession, but I hold that a saloon-keeper can be just as decent a man and as good a citizen as a butcher or store-keeper. Going to be with us long, Bill?"

"I don't know; I'm just rambling around. I might."

"I hope we can count on your vote if you're here. Look conditions over for yourself; they're terrible. This town is rotten to the core."

"Miss Molly's been explaining a bit."

"Molly is an ardent worker. So is Reverend Rutherford and his Nancy. And that reminds me, Molly—we're holding a meeting in the Gospel tent tonight at eight. Rutherford is going to the miners with the word and I wish you'd circulate around the stores and notify the ones we can count on. We want to select a candidate to take poor John's place. I'll be busy getting out the extra, but Fred has volunteered to ride out to all the ranches he can contact this afternoon and tell them about it."

"We're keeping the purpose of the meeting a secret, I suppose?"

"Yes. If Malone heard of it there's no telling what might happen."

Fred said, "I'd better be on my way; I have a lot of territory to cover."

"And I must get at my editorial," said Sexton.

"And you," said Bill to Molly, "must write your story." He got up. "I'll be ambling along, too; glad to have met you gentlemen."

Sexton nodded his acknowledgement and sat down at the other desk; Sivart gave Bill a nod and a smile and went out to the street. Bill leaned over Molly's desk and said solemnly, "Please, Miss Reporter, don't print anything about my burning the orphan asylum, will you? Lock it in your breast with the other privileged communications."

She frowned at him. "That was a mean trick, Bill—Bill Kringle. Now get out of here or somebody'll be writing your obituary."

ꜱ 3 ꜱ

Bill's Champion

ONCE outside, Borden got on his horse and rode to the *Frontier*. He tied and went inside; the members of Biff Bang's posse were lined up at the bar partaking of liquid consolation after their failure to save Sam Sneed.

As Bill passed the bartender he said, "Monk inside?" just as Biff Bang had said it. The bartender answered, "Yeah...Hey! What you want with him?"

"That's my business—and his," said Bill, and turned around the end of the bar. He rapped on the door, opened it, and went in.

Monk Malone was at his desk, and sitting in a chair across from him was the dandified gunman who was to have shot John Turner. They both stared at Bill and Monk Malone said, "What the hell do you want?"

"Just dropped in to pay my respects. You very busy?"

In addition to a big coarse face, Monk had a big, gross body. He didn't bother to keep that body tidy; his clothes were shabby and wrinkled and the string tie around the soiled collar was askew, with one end hanging outside his waistcoat. He said, "That's all, Smoke; tell him I'll take care of it."

Smoke Rafferty got up and went out through a door which opened on a passageway along the side of the saloon. He walked with small, mincing steps.

Monk scowled at Bill and said, "Well?"

Bill sat down in the chair Rafferty had vacated and pushed his hat back. He said, "I'm a stranger, just getting acquainted. Somebody told me you were the mayor, and I believe in starting at the top and working down."

"What handle you usin'?"

"Bill."

"Bill what?"

"Anything. That's it—Bill Anything."

Monk grunted. "Just what do you want with me?"

"Well, how about a job?"

"What kinda job?"

"Don't matter as l o n g as there ain't much work to it."

There was a sharp rap on the door, then it opened and Biff Bang stepped in. He closed the door, stood glaring at Bill, then said to Malone, "That's the bird that caught Sam."

Monk scowled at Bill. "That right, pilgrim?"

"Sure. You don't need to thank me; I'm modest."

"Thank you! Why you damned fool!" Malone stopped abruptly, glared for a second, then eased back in his chair and composed his face. "Just why did you horn in?" he asked in a voice that was ominously quiet.

"I told you I'm a stranger. I'd just rode into town and hadn't sized up the angles yet."

"And you got them angles sized up now?"

"Partly."

Without taking his eyes off Bill, Malone said to the marshal, "All right, Biff; beat it." Biff Bang went out into the bar room and closed the door.

Monk said, "And you want a job, huh? Ain't got no *dinero* and want to work your way, huh?" He paused a moment, then said sharply, "What you wanted for?"

"I kicked the stool from under a blind man and swiped his pennies."

Monk came to his feet, his eyes blazing. He leaned over the desk and shouted, "Don't get gay with me, *hombre!* I don't like it!"

Bill answered just as harshly, "Then don't ask personal questions! Think I spill my business to every stranger I meet?"

They glared at each other for a short space, then Monk sucked in his breath and slowly resumed his seat. The anger in his eyes died; he gave a grunt that was half chuckle. "You might do to take along, at that;

I dunno. There's nothin' open right now. Stick around and come to see me next week."

Bill sank back in his chair and fished out the making. "I'll stick. But I've got to find a place to hole up in."

"There's a few empty shacks around town; pick out one you like and take it. See you in a week."

"Keno," said Bill. He lighted the cigarette, then got up. "You handing me the key to the city?"

"I don't hand nobody nothin'. Step light and keep yore nose clean. And next time somebody gets salivated don't be so damned curious; we got a marshal to run down killers—when we want 'em run down. Get goin', Mister Anything."

Bill got going.

NOW THAT Borden had met Monk Malone, the situation in Calder was shaping up in his mind. Molly Sexton and her father and the Reverend Rutherford and his daughter had the courage of their convictions; but they were up against brains and brawn and bullets, plus organization, and a very understandable reluctance on the part of Monk Malone to surrender his authority and the income he enjoyed from the protection he offered fugitives from the law

Fugitives from the law. Bill glanced about him as he strode through the saloon and saw all about him those faces without names, as Molly Sexton had called them. Thieves, swindlers, crooked gamblers, killers; all gathered at Calder, all owing Malone for protection, ready to band together if the need arose to keep out meddling lawmen. Nothing short of a full company of Rangers would be able to ride into this town and clean it up properly.

Of course, if the reform party could win at the polls there would be nothing to it. Give them that boost and the doubters, the timid and the inert well-wishers would all pitch in and help wholeheartedly. But let them fail this once and they were licked forever, their prestige gone; they were staking everything on one throw and that wasn't good gambling.

Bill found an empty cabin and went to work on it. He bought a broom, a bucket and scrub brush, soap, and a couple yards of flannel. When he had finished with it, it was clean if nothing else. There was a rusty stove, and he cut some wood for it; he bought some candles, food and a sack of grain for his horse. He cooked and ate supper and felt at home.

When he had washed up his dishes, he put on a clean shirt and scarf and rode to the Gospel tent, which he had located while searching for a cabin. It was early, but he heard the strains of the melodion as he dismounted and tied outside the entrance, then went into the tent.

A quiet gloom hung over the covered space with its rows of plank benches, its small platform where a table served as pulpit, and the little melodion a bit off to one side. Bill removed his hat, trod softly down the earthen aisle and sat down on the front bench. Nancy Rutherford was playing something soft and sweet, improvising as she played. He could see her head and shoulders above the top of the small organ. Her golden hair was a halo, her eyes deep blue; she smiled at him and he smiled back and listened rapturously until the last chord swelled and then died.

Nancy came over to him and sat on the bench beside him.

He said, "Why did you stop? It was beautiful."

"I saw you were alone and thought maybe you'd rather talk. You're the man who caught Sam Sneed, aren't you?"

"Yes." He was grave.

Her face clouded. "It was dreadful; both the shooting of Mr. Turner and the hanging of Sam. It wasn't really Sam who killed Mr. Turner; the real murder has gone unpunished."

"Monk Malone?"

She shook her head at him. "It isn't for me to judge. I don't know. I do know that Sam wouldn't have killed Mr. Turner without orders from somebody. Are you planning to stay in Calder, Mister—?"

"Just call me Bill, Miss Rutherford. I don't think I'll stay, but I'll be here for a while.

"I hope you'll vote for the Cleanup Party; we're going to do big things for Calder, Bill."

"I sure hope you swing it and I'll do all I can to help; but you have a tough job ahead of you. If the law moved in first and chased out the roughs, you'd win hands down."

"What law we have in Calder is controlled by Monk Malone," she said sadly. "And the county sheriff is afraid to interfere. The Rangers are few and scattered and too busy with more important matters. We've tried to interest them; Mr. Sexton wrote the most urgent letters, and father wrote to the governor himself. All they got in return was the vague promise of help when the necessary force could be spared. No,. Bill, we must fight it out alone. And we're going to; we're going to win the election."

"I sure hope you do, Miss Rutherford."

"Call me Nancy; everybody does."

REVEREND Rutherford came through a flap at the back of the tent bearing a lighted kerosine flare. He hung this on a hook on the tent pole nearest the pulpit, then came over to join them. Bill stood up and Rutherford extended his hand. He smiled, and the smile transfigured his rugged face. "This is Bill, isn't it? Molly Sexton was telling me about you. Are you coming to the meeting?"

"I'll be around."

"Good. We need the support of every honest man and woman in the community. You'll excuse Nancy, won't you? I want her to help me select the hymns."

Bill said, "Of course," and they went over to the organ. While they bent over a hymn book Bill quietly went out. It was getting dark now, and he moved a short distance away and sat down on a saw horse near a wood pile. He rolled a cigarete and smoked it thoughtfully. This Nancy Rutherford was sure one fine girl; an evangelist's daughter she, too, was interested in the soul-saving—yet she hadn't mentioned religion to him once.

People began to arrive for the meeting. They came singly or in pairs, unobstrusively and most likely unobserved by Malone's crowd, who would naturally be as far away from the Gospel tent as they could get. Tradesmen with their wives and sons and daughters arrived on foot, as did the miners; cowboys arrived on horseback but not in bunches as was their usual wont. Apparently everybody had been cautioned against arousing the suspicion of Malone's outfit. Molly Sexton, her father, and Fred Sivart came together. Against the faint glow which came from within the tent Bill saw Rutherford standing in the entrance greeting each person as they arrived.

At last it was completely dark, and no more persons entered, Bill heard the deep voice of Reverend Rutherford as he asked the Lord to bless those who had gathered in the humble Temple and the cause for which they fought. Then came the strains of the organ and voices lifted in song. The hymn was a militant one, eminently fitting. It was "Onward, Christian Soldiers."

Bill heard the mumble of voices but could not distinguish the words. He guessed that the regular prayer meeting had been deferred in order that they might discuss the crisis caused by John Turner's death.

* * *

The attack came without warning. A band of horsemen swept suddenly from the void behind Bill, circling the wood pile and rushing towards the tent. One moment there had been silence; the next was a bedlam; hoofs pounded the earth, shrill yells ripped the air, sixguns thundered their contents through the canvas top of the tent. The riders circled like Indians attacking a wagon train; the canvas shook and heaved, and above the shouts sounded the cries of the frightened women inside. Then the whole front of the tent collapsed; somebody had roped the front pole and had torn it loose.

And the kerosene flare was attached to that pole.

Bill was already on his feet, his sixgun in his hand. He ran forward, firing at the figures that flashed by. He dropped one, saw a horse go down; then came a burst of flame as the canvas caught fire.

For an instant even the harsh cries of the raiders were stilled. The tent was begining to blaze and there were people trapped inside. That knowledge appalled even the callous roughs who were responsible; they reined away from the scene of a possible tragedy and faded into the darkness.

Cries came out of the terror and confusion within the tent; the half of the canvas nearest the entrance was still erect, and people began streaming out; but the half near the pulpit was down, coming to a peak some five feet from the ground where it was held up by the table on the platform. It was just in front of this bulge that the fire was leaping into the air.

Bill waded up the yielding canvas like a man in a sea of molasses. He thrust his sixgun into his holster and got out his clasp knife. He couldn't extinguish the fire; he could only keep it from spreading. He slashed away at the canvas, ripping it in a circle about the fire. By the time he had worked around to his starting point, his hands were scorched and his hair singed, but he had the satisfaction of seeing the blazing canvas fall to the earth and consume itself. The burning torch had fallen free of the hook and was lying on its side, still burning. Bill snatched it up by the handle and hurled it out on the empty lot, then ducked under the canvas and worked his way towards the melodion. He stumbled into it, found a match and thumbed it into flame and looked about him. Nancy was not here; she had evidently got out in time. He crawled under the pegged-down side wall and wriggled out into the fresh air.

There was as much confusion without as there had been within; women were gathered in a knot talking shrilly and angrily; men rushed about in the dark as though expecting to find the raiders hiding nearby; there was a small group gathered about the marauder whom Bill had shot, and another one about the stricken horse.

Cowboys milled about looking for the horses which the marauders had turned loose. Bill started off in search of his own mount. At the end of nearly an hour he found it in the alley near the *Frontier*, and guessed it had followed the retreating raiders to their rendezvous. He mounted and rode up the street.

THERE WAS a light in the *Clarion* office so Borden dismounted and went in.

Sexton and Rutherford, the two girls, and Fred Sivart were there, and as he entered. Molly turned and saw him. Her eyes were stormy and her face was white with anger.

She said furiously, "You certainly have gall to come here after what you've done!"

"And what," inquired Bill coldly, "am I supposed to have done?"

"You told Monk Malone about the meeting! You were probably right with the bunch that came near to burning us alive!"

He said roughly, "You're crazy as a coot!"

"Am I? Who else could have done it? Who else knew?"

Fred Sivart said, "You were the only outsider who knew, Bill; you went straight from here to the *Frontier* and one of our informers said you were with Malone in his office."

A slow anger stirred Borden; but for him this tragedy might have been a far greater one. All that was necessary to set them right was to tell his story and show his blistered hands, but Bill's stubborness rose up in him and he found he didn't give a hoot in hades for the credit which was his due.

"Sure I talked with Malone," he said harshly. "Who of you hasn't? I wanted to get the lowdown on Calder. I'd heard one side of the story; why shouldn't I go to Malone for the other? You're a bunch of fanatics butting your heads against a stone wall. Well, go ahead and butt; the loss of brains won't be very heavy."

Nancy came forward and, putting a hand on Bill's arm, turned to face them. "We have no right to judge," she told them. "None of us saw Bill with the raiders and news of the meeting could h a v e leaked out in some other way. Fred mentioned one of our informers; Malone probably has his. Personally, I don't believe it was Bill who betrayed us."

She glanced about her defiantly, then looked up at Borden. The anger left him and he smiled down at her; he reached out and patted her on the shoulder. "Thanks, Nancy. Don't you go butting your head against that wall. You have something inside it that you can't afford to lose."

He turned and went out into the dark street.

⌇ 4 ⌇

Warning

ILL rode down to Fred Sivart's *Double Eagle* and went inside. The *Double Eagle* was newer and more ornate than was the *Frontier* and seemed to be the gathering place for cowboys and miners. Bill bought a drink and was sipping at it when John Turner's foreman, the man called Wes, came up and stood beside him.

Wes said, "I didn't thank you for nabbin' that polecat for us; I'm doin' it now. The name is Wes Peters."

Bill shook hands. "Folks call me Bill. Shooting Turner from the roof was a lowdown trick. Sam Sneed sure must have had it in for him."

Wes swore. "The louse hardly knew John; he was planted there in case Smoke Rafferty gummed it up. Smoke bought a hoss from John a couple weeks ago and later claimed the critter had the heaves and wasn't fit to ride. It wasn't true, of course; Rafferty just wanted an excuse to pick a fight with John. John was the Cleanup Party's candidate for mayor and had a good following; Smoke aimed to make either a coward or a corpse of him. Well, John wasn't no coward. We boys aimed to see that he

got a square deal on the shootout, but we hadn't counted on somebody hidin' on the roof."

"What happens to Turner's ranch now?"

"He got a wife and four young kids. We'll run it for them, me and the boys; and if we ever get the goods on Malone we'll sure settle with him if we have to shoot our way through the *Frontier* to his office."

"No proof that Malone's behind all this, huh?"

"Not a lick. Everybody knows he's collectin' money for givin' thieves and killers protection, but nobody can prove it. No more'n we can prove it was him that planted Sam Sneed on the roof."

"Just before the shot was fired, somebody signaled with a handkerchief from the far side of the street. Could it have been Malone?"

"Signaled? You mean somebody gave Sam the order to shoot?" Wes was thoughtful. He shook his head. "It wasn't Malone; he was in the *Frontier*, I'd swear; he never stirs out of the place."

"When's the funeral?"

"Tomorrow afternoon at the ranch. I came in to get John's body and arrange with Parson Rutherford to conduct the services. I h e a r Monk's roughs tore down the tent and came near to burnin' the whole works."

Bill nodded. "The fire was put out in time to save it. If you're looking for Rutherford, I left him at the *Clarion* office a few minutes ago."

"Thanks; I'll be headin' that way, So long, Bill."

Wes went out and Borden finished his drink, got his horse and rode to the cabin. He put the animal in a small corral in back of the place, then went inside, lighted a candle and closed and barred the door. He pushed the table in a corner where he could not be observed through a window, sat down and got a wad of papers from his coat pocket. He smoothed these out and began reading them slowly and carefully.

They were notices describing men who were wanted for various crimes, and some of them had pictures of the men they described. Bill studied them, trying to match them up with the faces he had seen in Calder. Four of them, he was positive, were even then in the *Frontier*, members of Biff Bang's posse; and a fifth notice contained an accurate description of Biff himself. The protruding eyes were a dead giveaway; the man's name was Cleve Bangor and he was wanted for armed robbery and murder.

There was nothing on Monk Malone himself, which was a disappointment; if Monk were wanted by the law, Bill might manage to get him out of Calder and turn him over to the sheriff at the county seat. That would remove the core of the boil which was Calder. Making Monk a prisoner, surrounded as he was by gunmen and knife artists, would be a job in itself; to attempt it without any definite charge to pin on him would be utterly foolish. It was necessary to establish beyond doubt that Monk was aiding and abetting criminals before a move against him could be made.

A name on one of the notices caught and held Borden's attention, and he read the notice several times. Name Al Travis; age, 26; height, 5 feet 11 inches; weight, 175 pounds; color of hair, blonde; eyes blue. Six-inch knife scar on chest. There was no picture. Bank robbery and murder, twice over.

Why the name had attracted him, Bill did not know; the description would fit any of a dozen men in Calder. The name itself held no familiar ring, yet Bill's eyes returned to it and lingered on it.

He gave it up at last, pried up a floor board and put the notices under it and turned in. He lay in his bunk for some time thinking over his problem, analyzing his impressions. He had met the leaders of the cleanup movement and the man behind what Rutherford called "the forces of evil"; he had gauged the determination and ability of the Rutherfords and the Sextons and had had demonstrated to him the power of the machine they were bucking. Bill was no zealot and refused to contemplate conditions through rose-colored

glasses. He had been momentarily swayed by the enthusiasm and confidence of Molly Sexton and Nancy Rutherford, almost had been persuaded that the Cleanup Party would sweep all before it. Now, in sober contemplation, he didn't believe that to be true; fair fighters stood no chance against dirty ones, and Malone and his crowd knew every trick in the book—and were capable of inventing new ones where necessary.

No, the surest way to clean up Calder was by methods known to Bill and used by him before; it would be dangerous in the extreme and he would probably earn the hatred of both these fine young women and the decent people associated with them; but what he did could not hurt their cause and what they did might help him.

Having made this decision, Bill promptly fell asleep.

EXCEPT THAT the stores were closed, Sunday was like any other day in Calder; the saloons were wide open and heavily patronized. Bill strolled about the town, sizing up people, registering impressions, trying to match more faces and forms to the descriptions on the circulars. He glanced into the *Clarion* office as he was passing and saw Molly seated at her desk chewing on the end of a pencil. She looked up, saw him, and motioned for him to wait, then jumped up and came outside to meet him.

She put out her hand and said, "Shake, Bill."

Wonderingly he did so. She twisted his hand and saw the blisters on its back. She looked up and there was contrition on her face. "I'm sorry, Bill; sorry for what I said last night. It was you who cut away the burning canvas and saved the tent, wasn't it?"

"Nope. I got those burns lighting a cigarette."

"Bill, you're the nicest liar I've ever known. Come inside."

She drew him into the office and made him sit down by her desk. "Nancy said she thought it was you, and afterwards we found a man who saw you throw the flare out into the lot. To show you that I'm really sorry I'm going to tell you a closely-garded secret. At the office here last night, we picked Tom Harrigan to run for mayor in John Turner's place. He's a miner and a good citizen and his selection should go a long way towards getting the miners to vote. What do you think of it?"

"I think that Tom Harrigan will be the next shooting victim."

"They wouldn't dare!"

"Why not? Killing off the opposing leaders is always a good bet; and every death costs you a vote."

"But they don't know; they won't know until the last minute."

"That's the best time to pop him off; then the election'll go to Malone by default."

"Bill, you're the most discouraging person!"

"I know what you're up against; you're fighting thieves and killers who face arrest and conviction if they're rooted out of Calder. They're safe here because they're banded together and can make it so hot for the law that it wouldn't be worth the cost in lives to come in after them."

He got up and leaned over the desk. "Molly, you're too fine a girl to be mixed up in this rotten mess. You're going to see things that no decent girl should see; there'll be looting and shooting and mud and blood. Go away somewhere until this thing is settled."

"I wouldn't think of it. Dad's in this with his whole heart and soul and I'm in it with him. Did you see the extra we put out?"

"Yes. Fred Sivert tacked one up in the saloon. A fine tribute to John Turner and a swell condemnation of Sam Sneed, but nothing but vague hints that Monk Malone was behind the killing."

"I know; we have no proof, you know."

"You don't need proof that a tiger's dangerous; you know it. By the way, how come that your father isn't running on the Cleanup Party? Not that I'd like to see him the target for another Sam Sneed, but he's a good man and would make a good mayor."

"He's a newspaper man; he can put up a better fight for somebody else than he could for himself. And after Calder's cleaned up we'll be moving on to another town that needs us. I told you Dad was a crusader."

"Yeah, I know. I also know that the crusaders failed in their mission. But I sure wish you luck."

"Me? Aren't you with us?"

"The time'll probably come when you think I'm not. You were mistaken once; I hope your faith is stronger the next time."

"Bill, what do you mean?"

He considered for a moment, then said, "When you move into a house that's run down you begin your cleaning at the dirtiest spot. You don't dust the walls, and ceilings and then start shoveling out the fallen plaster and broken glass and other filth. I don't think you'll ever clean Calder through an election. You're going at this with a feather-duster instead of a pick and a shovel; me, I'm a pick and shovel man."

He said goodbye and left her sitting there frowning after him.

BORDEN got his horse and rode down to the gulch where most of the mining claims were located. A few miners were working, but most of them were idle. Bill inquired for and located Tom Harrigan's cabin. Tom was sitting on the porch smoking his pipe. Bill ground-anchored his horse and joined him.

"Folks call me Bill," he introduced himself. "I understand you're going to run for mayor in John Turner's place."

"Who told you?"

"Molly Sexton. I warned her that the other side might try to pull a John Turner on you; she couldn't see it. What do you think?"

Harrigan removed his pipe and stared at Bill. The stare was not a friendly one. "I reckon I can take care of myself."

"That's what Turner thought."

"You're a stranger; what business is it of yours?"

"The election? None. I'll not be in Calder long and local affairs don't interest me, except that some mighty fine people are apt to get hurt—and that includes anybody who runs against Malone. I didn't t h i n k it would hurt to warn you to keep your eyes open and your gun handy."

"I've kept alive over fifty years by doin' just that, my friend. I don't reckon I need any warnin' from you or anybody else."

Bill got up. "Sorry I bothered you. You live alone?"

"Yes."

"Good. John Turner left a wife and four kids. Well, so long, Harrigan. Maybe you don't need the advice, but keep it in mind anyhow."

He rode away with the knowledge that while Tom Harrigan might be a good man he was also a stubborn one; he quite evidently resented advice from a man but half his age.

Bill did not go to John Turner's funeral. Most of the tradespeople did, some of them trying to slip out of town without being observed lest they incur Malone's enmity. Bill was ambling around town when Sivart drove up to a little house near the *Clarion* office in a shining new buggy. Molly came out and Fred helped her to the seat. She saw Bill and waved, and Sivart nodded and got in the buggy beside her. They drove away and presently Molly's father appeared in another buggy and set out in the same direction. Bill returned to the cabin and went over the wanted notices again; he had identified two more fugitives from the law, but Al Travis still refused to reveal himself.

The uproar came rolling into the cabin like a tidal wave. It was in the form of hoarse yells and pistol shots. Bill hurriedly put away the notices and went out. He didn't waste time in saddling his horse, but ran to the main street. There was a mob milling about the general store, and Borden walked swiftly towards the place, keeping on the far side of the street. The storekeeper, Henry Hollister, had gone to Turner's funeral.

The door to the building had been battered down and the big front window panes smashed. Inside the store, men were running about, tearing goods from shelves and counters and scattering them about. A rough was nailing a placard beside the broken door, but at the distance Bill could not see the words printed on it.

There wasn't anything he could do had he wanted to, and the whole thing came to an end within a matter of minutes. Marshal Biff Bang came running along the street brandishing his gun and shooting it into the air, and the roughs beat a precipitate retreat as though very much scared of him—which in itself was a bit ridiculous. Biff came up panting and swearing; he surveyed the damage from the outside, then, gun in hand, went into the store and poked about. Apparently satisfied that there was nobody hidden there, he came out and seated himself on the steps, the faithful mastiff mounting guard over his dead master's grave.

Bill grinned and crossed the street. He stood in front of the steps reading the placard. In large letters was printed MALONE FOR MAYOR, and beneath this, in smaller letters, *Business is good. Keep it that way.* It was a hand job and a good one, with the letters evenly formed and spaced and the words correctly spelled. Not, thought Bill, the work of Monk Malone.

Biff Bang said, "Move along, pilgrim; excitement's over."

"Ended by the arrival of our valiant marshal. It was a good show, Cleve."

Biff's eyes popped. "The name is Cliff. Cliff Bang."

"The name," said Bill calmly, "is Cleve. Cleve Bangor."

The marshal's hand moved towards the Colt which had been returned to its holster, but stopped half way there. Bill had made no move, but his steady gaze was on Biff and the latter decided not to risk it sitting down.

He waved the hand in a dismissing gesture. "Call me anything you like, pilgrim, just so's you're happy."

"I'll call you Biff in public," promised Bill. "I wouldn't embarrass you for the world."

"Where'd you get hold of that name you spoke?"

"Read it somewhere; and it wasn't in the Bible."

Borden moved to the wall of the building and stood with his back to it while he rolled a cigarette. Biff Bang, or Cleve Bangor, was on his left; Bill could draw and shoot across his own body if necessary, and the marshal was in too awkward a position to try anything. Bangor watched Bill steadily as the latter made the cigarette and lighted it. There was speculation and doubt in the marshal's pop eyes. Bill worked gradually to his right until he came to the corner of the store, then said, "So long, Cleve," and slipped into the passageway and back to the alley.

He had given the enemy something to think about. He had made the first move in the game he expected to play.

∫ 5 ∫

The Job

THERE was a great deal of righteous wrath on the part of Hank Hollister over the damage to his property, but there was nothing he could do about it except thank Biff Bang for preventing any further destruction. Grudgingly, he thanked the marshal knowing that had looting been intended, Biff's presence would have made no difference. Nobody could be found to identify the marauders, which is not so strange when it is considered that those who would have been willing to identify them were absent at the funeral. Bill blamed the attack on a bunch of drunks who were having what was their idea of fun.

Hank didn't protest too much; he put up a new door and glass in the window and called himself lucky for getting off so easy. He had read the placard and recognized it for the warning it was. Business was good and he wanted to keep it that way; to keep it that way, he gathered, he should vote for Monk Malone.

Nothing upsetting happened during the next few days. The Sextons were busy getting out that week's paper, which was issued on Thursday. The Rutherfords held their regular meetings in a tent which had been patched and erected again, but the attendance would have discouraged anybody but the parson and his daughter.

On Tuesday night they held a special service for the miners, transporting the organ to the gulch, where the earth furnished seats and the star-studded sky a canopy. Undoubtedly that meeting gave the campaign of the Cleanup Party a big boost, for when the service was over Nancy sat for two hours playing and singing for the men. There were songs of home and waiting sweethearts that brought tears to the eyes of many a hardbitten miner, and there were songs like "Suzanna" in which they joined, stamping their feet to keep time.

Bill Borden just loafed about town, apparently taking life easy; but he knew that in recognizing Cleve Bangor he had started something and was prepared to meet whatever came up. If Biff reported to Malone that Bill had identified him as Cleve Bangor, the powers that be might decide that Bill was a lawman, in which case there would be a speedy and perhaps disastrous show-down. As the days passed uneventfully, Bill decided that Biff had kept his knowledge to himself and would act on his own responsibility if he thought any action was necessary.

The paper came out on Thursday and Bill bought a copy at the store and took it home to read. There was the expected editorial on vandalism, inspired by the raid on Hollister's store, but Malone was not named as its instigator. Bill met Molly on the street the next day and walked to the office with her. "I see you're still using that feather duster," he told her.

"What do you mean?"

"That editorial. You had the chance to lay Monk Malone out and you muffed it; instead of laying the blame right at his door where it belonged, you went into a tirade against conditions in general, which everybody already knows are awful."

"But we couldn't name Malone; as usual, we have no proof."

"Afraid he'll sue you for libel?"

"He could."

"He won't; he'd have to sue in the county court and that's one piece of machinery Monk isn't going to monkey with. Better start using that pick and shovel."

"You're the pick and shovel man," she told him tartly. "You said so yourself. But I haven't seen any huge piles of *debris* being carted away."

"I'm a slow starter; but when I get started the dirt'll fly."

"Put off starting for two more weeks and we'll do the job for you —at the polls. I guess you read about the meeting in the gulch? We'll have every miner down there voting for Tom Harrigan. And that reminds me, Mister Smarty; the name of our candidate is still a secret."

"Want to bet?"

"Certainly! Only seven of us know it. Dad and myself, Reverend Rutherford and Nancy, Fred Sivart and you, and Tom himself."

"I hope you're right, but I wouldn't bank on it. I'd lay a good-sized bet right now that Malone knows. And I'd lay one twice as large that you'll never clean up Calder at the polls; they're too smart for you, too ruthless, too dirty."

"I'll take both bets. And if I should lose, we'll sell the *Clarion* to pay off."

SATURDAY came, and with it the expiration of the week Bill was to wait before seeing Malone again. He went down town shortly before noon and got a surprise; across the front of the *Frontier* was stretched a strip of canvas and on it was painted in crude but large letters FREE DRINKS FOR MINERS.

It was Malone's answer to Rutherford's special service in the gulch.

Bill went inside and bought a drink. There were not many customers; it was still early. Biff Bang was at the end of the bar and saw Bill enter. He went into Malone's office, then came out almost at once and beckoned to Bill. Bill finished his drink and followed him into the office. Monk was behind his desk. Biff stood with his back to the closed door and Malone motioned towards a chair. Bill picked it up and carried it over to the wall, then sat down. Monk raised an eyebrow in question and Bill said, "I have good ears; I can hear you from over here."

Malone said, "You still want that job?"

"Yes."

"Well, I got a little one to start you on. If you handle it right I maybe can find somethin' permanent for you. You seen our sign? Well, we'll have a flock of miners in here tonight; they'll get drunk and likely raise Cain. Biff's gonna need somebody to help him keep order; you're it."

Bill rubbed his chin thoughtfully. "I'm the law, huh?"

"You're a hunk of it. Biff'll tell you what he wants done. Anything he says goes; do as he tells you and you're settin' pretty. That's all."

Bill got up and turned to Biff. The marshal produced a deputy's badge.

"Pin it on you somewhere and report to me after supper."

That was all there was to it, but Bill seethed with anticipation; something was in the wind for that night and he was in on it. He couldn't guess what it was to be; he'd have to play them close to his chest and use his judgment. It was the kind of job Borden liked; he pinned the badge on the inside of his coat and followed Biff from the room.

He went home, had dinner, and came back downtown in the middle of the afternoon. Calder was filling up and miners were flocking to the *Frontier*, drawn by the sign. Bill went into the *Double Eagle*. There were some cowboys here, but the only miner he saw was Tom Harrigan, and Tom kept glancing across the street, temptation tugging at him.

Fred Sivart was standing at the end of the bar and Bill said to him, "You'll have to put up a bigger sign offering bigger free drinks."

Sivart smiled wryly. "Looks like it, doesn't it? Especially if I want to go broke. Those boys from the gulch drink like so many fishes."

BILL STROLLED about town and finally met Molly Sexton coming out of the store. He tipped his hat to her and she stopped for a moment.

"Pick and shovel still idle," she reproved. "Bill, I do believe you're a lazy workman."

"Just a mite slow starting, that's all; I'm limbering up. Want an item for next week's paper?" He turned back his coat and showed her the badge.

"Bill! Where did you get that?"

"From Biff Bang, our noble marshal. Am I proud!"

There was hurt in her dark eyes. "Bill, you haven't! You haven't gone over to—to the other side!"

"I'm on the side of law and order; the badge proves it. And don't let your woman's intuition run away with you—it did once, you know. Maybe I'd better take it up to Nancy Rutherford and show it to her."

"But, Bill, what does it mean?"

"I don't know—yet. But I will tonight. Be seein' you."

He moved away before she could ask any more questions, and she gazed after him with a puzzled look on her face until the crowd had swallowed him. Then she shook her head and went her way.

He ate supper at a restaurant to save the trouble of preparing a meal, and when he had finished, walked back to the *Double Eagle*. Wes and the boys from the Turner ranch had come in, and presently Borden found an opportunity to talk to Peters alone.

He said, "Wes, I know you're honing to get back at Monk Malone. I'm going after him myself but I got to do it in a way that most folks won't understand. Keep it under your hat; don't mention it to anybody. I'm telling you because when I need help I'll probably need it bad and fast; I'm counting on you and your boys."

Wes gave him a long look. "We'll be around. Day or night."

Bill left it at that. Somewhere in the ranks of the Cleanup Party was an informer, and he didn't want to be seen talking too long to the cowman.

Tom Harrigan had substituted whiskey for supper, and the urge to join his fellows in the *Frontier* was getting stronger. He finally went out and crossed the street and went into Malone's saloon. Bill followed him.

The *Frontier* was all noise and movement; men were lined up at the bar three deep and the games were running full out. Girls circulated among the crowd, soliciting drinks and gambling-stakes. Harrigan elbowed his way to the bar, and Bill joined Biff Bang, who was seated in a tilted chair at the far end of the gaming tables. Bill sat down beside him and said, "Deputy reporting for duty, Sir."

Biff was looking intently towards the bar. He said from the corner of his mouth, "Get this and get it right. We're after one of them miners. We're goin' to put him out of business—permanent. Not now; the crowd's too thick. But pretty soon the fiddle and piano will strike up a dance. Them miners are suckers for dancin'. One of 'em ain't gonna dance. That's your part of the play, to keep him at the bar. Git into an argument, then tell him he's under arrest and flash your badge. He's Irish and drunk and he'll want to fight. Egg him on to drawin'; I'll do the rest."

Bill felt his back hair begin to prickle. He said, "What do you mean you'll do the rest? If the danged fool goes for his gun what do I do?"

"Nothin'. Let him draw. I'll be at this end of the bar and I'll feed it to him. Resistin' arrest. By not drawin', you're in the clear; makes it look better. Get it?"

BORDEN GOT it, but not exactly the way Biff intended him to He saw at once that if Biff had any fear of him, of his knowledge of Biff's identity, this would be a good way of getting rid of him without risk to the marshal. All Biff had to do was hold his fire and let the miner blast away at Bill. Exit Bill Borden. Pretty good.

Bill said, "I got it. I let him draw and you plug him before he gets me. That means I must be between him and the door. Keno. Who is he?"

"Tell you in a minute; he's hid in the crowd right now."

On the little stage a fiddler began to tune up. Some of the miners turned to look expectantly that way. There was a short pause, then piano and fiddle struck up a lively tune and the bunch at the bar began to dissolve. Miners gulped their drinks, seized the girls nearest to them and dragged them to the small dance floor; when the supply of girls ran out, miners paired up with each other. The three ranks in front of the bar became two, became one, became five or six scattered individuals.

Biff got up, his pop eyes staring and his jaws were tightly clamped. He made a quick motion to Bill and Bill got up also.

Biff said, "There he is—the feller in the middle, just takin' a drink."

The man was Tom Harrigan.

So Malone *did* know about Tom's candidacy! And Bill's prediction that Tom would be the next shooting victim was about to be fulfilled. Unless—

Sure it had to be stopped, but how? He could think of no way at the moment, didn't even want to. Borden's mind worked best in the thick of action. He said, "Keno!" and started across the floor.

As he stepped to the bar beside Harrigan, Tom looked at him and said, "You, huh?" He was the type that turns surly and suspicious when drinking.

"Who'd you think I was—Santa Claus?" said Bill harshly.

"Smarty pants!" sneered Harrigan. "The li'l boy that passes out warnin's."

"You're drunk."

"Whozh drunk?' blazed Harrigan. "I can drink three smarty pants like you under the table."

He raised his glass and Bill jostled his elbow, causing him to spill some of the liquor. "What did I tell you?" sneered Borden. "Drunk as a hoot owl."

He glanced past Harrigan. Biff was standing near the end of the bar, his feet spread and braced, his right arm crooked. Looked like he really meant to shoot.

Harrigan swore thickly and threw the rest of the drink in Bill's face. By turning his head in time, Bill got it on the cheek instead of in the eyes. Then Harrigan cut loose with a haymaker which, had it landed, must have knocked Bill into the next county. It didn't land; Bill leaped backwards and to his right and Harrigan, carried by the momentum, lurched away from the bar.

Bill snapped, "Hold it, you! You're under arrest!" He pulled back his coat, flashing the badge. He was looking at Harrigan but he could see Biff Bang beyond him. Biff's fingers were on his gun butt and he was ready to pull; but Biff's eyes were not on Harrigan, they were watching Bill.

And in that instant Bill knew what he had to do.

Harrigan yelled, "Arrest, hell!" and clawed at his gun. Bill's hand went to the butt of his own Colt. He seemed to be watching Harrigan, but in reality he was watching the marshal; he saw Biff's gun leap into his hand and swing around. And Biff was still looking directly at Borden.

Bill leaped sideways three feet, and in the next instant several things happened. Harrigan, reactions slowed by drink, got his gun momentarily hung in its holster; Biff fired and the slug tugged at Bill's left sleeve; Bill tilted the swivel holster upward and fired through its open bottom.

He fired just the one shot, then leaped forward and let Harrigan have a right that thudded solidly against the Irishman's chin. Harrigan staggered back a step, tangled his feet and sat down with a thump. He sat there staring, partly sobered, marveling that he was still alive.

Beyond Harrigan, Biff was staggering towards the bar. The marshal dropped his gun and his knees sagged beneath him; he gripped the edge of the bar with both hands, trying to pull himself erect. Biff didn't have the strength; his body went suddenly limp and he collapsed at the foot of the bar.

The music had stopped and the dancers were staring. The men who had been at the bar were there no more; some were behind it, some were under gaming tables.

Bill walked over to Harrigan, grasped him by the coat lapels and hauled him to his feet. "Sober now?"

Harrigan nodded, dumbly.

"That being the case, the arrest is off. Get out of here fast and stay out; and maybe now you'll listen to little smarty pants."

Bill walked around the staring Harrigan and bent over the marshal; Biff was quite dead. Bill straightened and said to the bartender, "Monk inside?"

The man nodded, his jaw sagging. Bill knocked once on the door and went in.

∫ 6 ∫

Reactions

MONK was seated behind his desk; Smoke Rafferty stood by a chair near the wall, poised and ready for action; Bill concluded that Rafferty was Monk's personal bodyguard.

Borden closed the door and Monk said, "What's up? Where's Biff?"

"Send your bloodhound back into the dog house and I'll tell you."

Monk said, "Set down, Smoke; this feller was workin' with Biff."

Rafferty sat down and Malone said to Bill, "I asked you where's Biff? What was the shootin' out there?"

Bill ignored both questions. He said, "Malone, what's the idea of trying to frame me?"

Monk's eyebrow went up. "What you talkin' about?"

"You heard me." Bill walked over to the desk and leaned his weight on it, looking down at Monk Malone but also watching Smoke Rafferty. "You

know the setup. Biff and I were to get Tom Harrigan between us. I was to make him draw and Biff was to plug him. Right?"

"You're doin' the talkin'. If that's what Biff told you to do, it was up to you to do it."

"That was the setup, all right; but when Harrigan made his play, Biff fired at me instead of at Tom. He missed and I plugged him. I don't reckon Biff'd do that without orders; that's why I'm asking why you tried to frame me."

Malone was genuinely astonished. "You givin' it to me straight?"

Bill indicated the tear in his coat sleeve. "What does that look like?"

"Sure it wasn't Harrigan done that?"

"Harrigan never got his gun clear. I knocked him down before he could draw. Ask anybody; they all saw it."

Monk stared at him, then at Rafferty. "Why, the double-crossin' polecat! What in the name of blazes made him pull a stunt like that?"

"That," said Bill grimly, "is what I'm asking you."

"Dang it! I had nothin' to do with it! The idea was to get Harrigan. This here cleanup outfit's named him their candidate; now Biff's gummed the works and it all gotta be done over again. Serves him danged good and right; fellers like him oughta get plugged."

Bill straightened slowly and took a deep breath. "Sounds all right. Maybe you didn't order it that way, but I wondered. I wondered because you picked me for the job instead of somebody like Rafferty."

"We're savin' Smoke," Malone told him. "We picked you because you wanted a job and we hadda try you out first."

"Well, I been tried out. Like lard. What now?"

Malone hesitated. He seemed uncertain. He glanced at Rafferty, wet his lips, looked back at Bill. "I—I dunno. I gotta think things over. You stick around; we'll find somethin' for you. Somethin' good. You stick around."

"Keno. But don't make me stick too long. I just shot your town marshal and if you don't want more of your crowd laid up, you'd better tell them the whys and wherefores. I'll be around when you want me."

He backed to the door and went out quickly.

The noise in the *Frontier* was subdued. The shooting of a man was nothing new to Calder, but in this case folk were puzzled. Biff was a Malone man, which should have meant that his deputy was also; yet the deputy had shot the marshal. It all appeared as a frameup against Harrigan, but in some manner it had gone wrong. If the deputy had missed Harrigan and hit Biff, that was an accident and Malone's men had no grounds for action against Bill; if it had been deliberate, the miners certainly had no quarrel with the deputy. It was all very puzzling.

Biff lay where he had fallen. Bill glanced about the room and saw the bewilderment on faces and knew that for the moment he had nothing to fear from either side. He started for the door, walking briskly.

A bartender called after him, "Hey, Deputy! What'll we do with Biff?"

Bill answered over his shoulder. "Don't ask me; it's not my joint. Toss him into the alley if you feel like it."

BORDEN WENT out to find a small crowd collected about the entrance; some had crossed from the *Double Eagle,* among them Fred Sivart and Wes Peters. Bill turned right and started along the street and the two men followed him. The street was lighted only where flares above doorways pushed back the shadows or faint illumination filtered through windows; at a dark spot Bill halted and waited for them to join him.

Sivart said, "What happened, Bill? Don't tell me they got Harrigan!"

"Harrigan's all right. Biff tried to get me and I shot first."

"You got Biff!" Sivart was incredulous. "But why should Biff try to kill you? Was it because he thought you were working under cover for the Cleanup Party?"

"He tried to kill me because I recognized him as Cleve Bangor, wanted for armed robbery and murder."

Wes said, "Good for you! That makes one less skunk runnin' loose."

Fred Sivart said, "I'll say it does! Bill, you're good; really good. The Cleanup Party needs more men like you. How are Malone's men taking it?"

"They haven't figured it out yet."

"Guess I'd better go inside and find out what happens. I don't usually patronize the *Frontier,* but there's no law against it. You coming along, Wes?"

"No. I ain't a bit curious. Some of Biff's friends might try to get even with Bill, and if they do I don't want to miss the fun."

Sivart turned back and Borden and Wes continued along the street. Wes said, "Bill, I'd like to get in on the ground floor with you. You got me puzzled. I trust you, yes; but I'd like to know your game. How come you were Biff's deputy to begin with?"

"I've told you about all I can, Wes, and it's strictly between you and me. I want to help the Cleanup Party, but I think they're going at things the wrong way. I'm used to fighting fire with fire. I asked Malone for a job and he gave me this one. Maybe Biff asked him to so that he could get me—it doesn't matter. I got a toehold on the inside, which is where I want to be."

"You don't have to tell me any more. All I ask is that you give me and the boys a chance to help. John Turner was a white man."

"You'll have that chance. You do just as I ask without questions and you'll be in at the finish. How far is it to the Turner ranch?"

"Not more'n an hour's ride, if you're in a hurry."

"Could you come to town every night after supper?"

"I sure can."

"Be at the *Double Eagle,* but leave it to me to get in touch with you. We don't want to appear too friendly from here on. Malone had an uncanny way of finding out things, maybe by that fellow who signaled to Sam Sneed with the handkerchief, whoever he is." He considered for a moment. "You got a strong outbuilding on the ranch?"

"We got a stable built of logs. It's dark inside and the roof ain't much, but it's strong."

"Fix it up with stout doors that can be barred on the outside, will you?"

"I sure will." Wes looked curious, but he did not question.

THEY SEPARATED and Bill walked up the street to the end of town. He could see the glow of light inside the Gospel tent and he heard the strains of the melodeon as Nancy practiced the evening's hymns. Bill went in. He liked to talk with Nancy. He sat down on the front bench and when she recognized him she stopped playing and joined him.

"I haven't seen you for days, Bill," she told him in her quiet voice. "I was hoping you'd stop in. What have you been doing?"

"Not much, Nancy. Not until tonight. I heard about the special meeting for the miners. It was a grand idea. But, Nancy, you *must* persuade Tom Harrigan to keep under cover until after election. He was framed tonight and they nearly got him. They know he becomes quarrelsome when he's drinking, and it's so easy to start a fight with him. They'll get him sure if he doesn't watch his step."

Nancy was frowning in worriment. "You say they nearly got him; how?"

Before he could tell her they heard someone come in the tent and turned their heads. It was too gloomy to see who it was, but Molly Sexton's voice called, "Nancy?" Then she recognized Bill and said, "Oh! Excuse me. A special meeting of some kind?"

Nancy said, "Come here, Molly. Bill just told me that Tom Harrigan was in some sort of trouble tonight and I asked him what it was."

Excitement shone in Molly's face and she was breathing quickly as though she had hurried. She sat down beside them, perching on the edge of the plank, tense and alert.

"He should have plenty to tell," she said. "Bill, let's have the straight of it; how did you happen to kill Marshal Bang?"

Nancy gave an exclamation. "Kill? Marshal Bang? *Bill?*"

"Yes, Bill. The whole town's talking about it. That's what I came to tell you. How did it happen, Bill?"

"Well," drawled Bill, "it wasn't much. Biff had two sixguns, a shotgun and a knife. I just—"

She made an impatient gesture. "I know. You picked him up by an ankle and waved him around your head. That was Sam Sneed; I'm talking about Biff."

Nancy looked at Bill and there was distress in her blue eyes. "Bill, you didn't really kill him, did you?"

He couldn't joke with her. "I had to, Nancy. Malone called me into his office this afternoon and asked me if I wanted to help Biff keep order tonight. I said I did and Biff made me his deputy. Tonight Harrigan was drunk; he got into a quarrel with me and when I tried to arrest him he went for his gun. Biff was behind him; he drew and fired, but not at Harrigan; Biff shot at me. I saw him just in time and jumped. I had to shoot him."

"Bill, you're the most amazing man," declared Molly. "I don't get it at all. Biff appoints you his deputy, then tries to shoot you; it doesn't make sense."

"Maybe he shot at Tom and missed," offered Bill.

"At twenty feet? Think up a better one."

"Well, maybe he didn't like the color of my hair."

Nancy was plainly distressed. She shook her head sadly. "It's wicked; it's wrong to kill anybody under any circumstances. Oh, why do men have to settle every question with guns? Why can't they sit down and talk things over, or thresh them out in the courts?"

Molly said, "A fine chance Bill had to sit down and talk things over with Biff throwing lead at him!"

"It's still wrong."

"I reckon most of us would rather be wrong and alive than right and dead," Bill told her. "I didn't enjoy shooting Biff; but it may make you feel better when I tell you that Biff's real name was Cleve Bangor and that he was wanted by the law for armed robbery and murder."

"Now I get it!" cried Molly. "You recognized him and he knew it, so he tried to shoot you."

"You hold your horses," Bill told her sternly. "That's not for publication. Lock it in your breast with those other privileged communications."

"But, Bill, it'd make such good copy! Mayor Malone's marshal a criminal, a murderer! More votes for the Cleanup Party!"

"You print that and I'll take your plant apart, piece by piece."

"All right. Don't bite me. What were you going to tell Nancy about Tom Harrigan?"

TELLING Nancy was entirely different from telling Molly. Molly's zeal might prompt her to print something which would lead Monk Malone to suspect that Biff's deputy had been talking out of turn. That would end the tieup with Malone and Borden was depending on that tieup to worm himself into Monk's organization. It was the only way of securing the information he needed, and it would be dangerous enough as it was.

"Tom was right between me and Biff," he evaded. "Biff could easily have shot him when he went for his gun."

"But he didn't; he shot at you. And besides, why Harrigan?"

"Because they know he's your candidate for Mayor."

"But, Bill, that's impossible. Only seven—"

"I know. Only seven of us are in the secret, so you think. You told me; maybe somebody else told a friend of his. Maybe Tom himself told." He got up. "I've got to go down town. So far as I know I'm Biff's only deputy; that makes me the law in Calder. Treat me with the proper respect."

Molly got up also. "I don't know how to treat you. One moment I think you're for us, and the next I'm sure you're against us. Would your Majesty deign to permit a humble reporter to walk as far as the office with you?"

Bill said he reckoned his majesty could stand it, and they left the tent together. They walked in silence for some distance, then Molly said, "That was a frameup against Tom Harrigan and you were a party to it."

"What makes you think that?"

"It has all the earmarks. You were to arrest Harrigan knowing he'd put up a fight, and Biff was to shoot him for resisting arrest."

"I told you Biff shot at me."

"I heard you. But suppose he had shot at Harrigan?"

"I didn't aim to let Tom get hurt. Knowing Biff was a murderer, I'd have winged him first."

"And what would you have told your boss?"

"Malone? I'd have said that I thought Biff was aiming at me."

"You're rather careless with the truth, aren't you, Bill? Even with me. I never know when to believe you; I don't know at this minute whose side you're on. Certainly if you went into that frameup with your eyes open you belong with the other thugs on Malone's side."

"I always go into things with my eyes open; it's you who're blind. Remember the Gospel tent."

They had come to the *Clarion* office and had halted. She put her hand on his arm and when she spoke again her voice was repentant. "I know, Bill. Forgive me. The way things leak out just gets me."

"Your outfit isn't careful enough. In your enthusiasm you talk, and somebody is carrying every word you say to Malone."

"I guess you're right. We'll have to be more careful." She stood for a moment thinking, then said, "I told father what you thought about his editorials. We're going to change with the next issue. We're going to come right out and lay the blame on Malone and accuse him openly of harboring criminals. Then we're going to send copies of the paper to the Governor, the County Attorney, and the Sheriff. If Malone sues us, at least the whole miserable mess will be dragged into the open. And that's something for you to lock in your breast as a privileged communication."

"Now you're talking! Monk won't sue. I'll make another bet with you on that."

"No you won't; you're too often right. All except the election. I'd bet the *Clarion* on our winning that."

"Well, I haven't much money, but I have plenty of time. I'll bet a lifetime of service against the *Clarion*. If the Cleanup Party wins the election you can order me around for the rest of my life."

"Done!" she said.

They shook hands on it.

7

Sixgun Religion

BORDEN went down the street, the people he passed eyeing him curiously. They didn't know where he stood and that was not to his liking. Straddling the fence is always a dangerous game, with the prospect of both sides turning against you ever present. He had been tossed into the thing before he had a chance to get his bearings; now he was faced with the problem of protecting Molly and Nancy and their friends, and at the same time apparently giving his all for Monk Malone.

He went into the *Frontier* and stood looking about him. The place was humming again, with the two-piece orchestra going full blast and miners lumbering about the dancing floor like so many grizzly bears; the air thick with dust and smoke. Biff's body had been removed. Bill went to the bar and was having a drink when Malone's office door opened and Smoke Rafferty came cut; the gunman surveyed the crowd and when he saw Bill he crooked a finger at him and jerked his head towards the office.

Bill finished his drink and followed Smoke inside. There were three other men present in addition to Malone.

Monk said, "Howdy, Bill. Meet up with Ed Dillon, Frank Cade and Pete Stacy. Ed runs the *Lucky Tiger;* Frank banks faro in the *Double Eagle,* and Pete owns the livery corral. The three of 'em make up the town council and I got 'em together at once because of Biff's checkin' out."

Bill nodded to them and got nods in return. Ed Dillon was a big surly man with a luxurious mustache, plastered-down hair and a perpetual scowl; Frank Cade looked like the gambler he was; Pete Stacy had associated with horses so long that he had come to look and smell like one. He had a long face, sad eyes, and a forelock that dangled over the bridge of his nose.

"The boys," said Monk, "have voted to put you in as marshal. Salary is a hundred a month. Suit you?"

"It'll do. I work alone?"

"Mostly. If you need help you come to me. I'll find you a deputy that'll serve without pay." He indicated a badge and a bunch of keys which lay on his desk. "Jail's alongside Ed's place. Nobody in it right now. Across the street from it is Judge Hibgy's office; he's our J. P. When you pull anybody in, run 'em over to the judge's and he'll try 'em."

Monk filled a tumbler half full of whiskey from the bottle on his desk, downed it in one gulp, then pushed bottle and glass towards Dillon. "Have a drink to the new town marshal, boys"

They drank in turn. Bill took his direct from the bottle; he didn't know much about germs but he doubted that even the rotgut liquor could kill the kind that Dillon and Stacy bred. Frank Cade, the gambler, was outwardly clean.

"Reckon that'll be all, boys," said Monk pointedly, and the three councilmen got up, shook hands with Bill and went out; at a signal from Monk, Rafferty went out with them.

Monk said, "Set down, Bill. Got a little business to talk over."

When Bill had straddled a chair, he went on. "You come to Calder for protection. That protection's gonna cost you somethin', naturally; you'll kick back half of that hundred bucks to me."

"Says who?"

"Says me. Feller like you can get along fine on fifty bucks a month and no worries. And they's plenty comin' in on the side; you run 'em in and get twenty-five percent of the fines. Runs into money."

"Who gets the other seventy-five percent?"

"Higby gets twenty-five and the organization gets fifty."

"Don't leave much for the town, does it?"

"Town don't need no money. No sewers or street pavin' to lay or other fancy things. Merchants chip in to pay your salary—and mine."

"What does the organization need money for?"

"You'll find out if a sheriff's posse ever rides into town. That dinero will hire enough guns to lick the United States Army and part of the Navy."

BILL GOT up, took the marshal's shield and pinned it where the deputy's badge had been, then put the latter and the keys in his pocket.

Monk said, "Hear you're right chummy with the Cleanup boys and gals. Well, that's all right as a bluff; you might hear somethin' we'd like to know. Looks better, too, your bein' marshal; shows we ain't playin' no politics where the good of the town's concerned."

He grinned, his thick lips parting to show two rows of stained teeth.

Bill said, "I know them to speak to and that's about all."

"Yeah? That Nancy gal is sure some dish, ain't she? Too bad she's so danged religious. And Molly Sexton ain't too bad, only you ain't got no chance there; Fred Sivart's got her corralled and ready for brandin'. Nice feller, Fred, even if he has throwed in with the other side. It's her doin's, of course. Well, good huntin'."

Bill said he hoped so and went out. Smoke Rafferty was at the end of the bar and Bill stepped up beside him and ordered a drink. Rafferty turned back Bill's coat and glanced at the badge. "So they made you marhsal. Right proud, ain't you?"

"Not too proud. All that shield means to me is grief."

"And a hundred bucks a month."

"Minus fifty."

"Plus protection. But that protection is only against outsiders. In Calder you step light. Don't start trampin' on any toes. Biff had a lot of friends; I'm one of them."

"Don't let grief over his untimely passing carry you too far."

Borden had all the advantage at the moment. He was on Rafferty's right and Smoke would have to step back before he could draw; Bill could simply pivot, tilt that swivel-holster and let go. He picked up his drink with his left hand, downed it, passed behind Rafferty and walked towards the door. Rafferty would not shoot him in the back; Smoke was proud of his ability with a sixgun, and would scorn to take advantage.

Bill went up the busy street, weaving through the crowd until he reached the *Clarion* office. Molly was at her desk working by the light of a lamp. He pushed open the door and thrust his head inside."

"Item for the paper," he said. "I been promoted. Hundred a month and reservations on Boothill." He pulled back his coat. "Ain't it pretty?"

He got a kick out of the surprise which flashed in Molly's eyes. The surprised look changed to a frown; she got up and came over to the door. "That does it," she said. "You've thrown in with them, haven't you?"

"You don't like it? Heck, the town council elected me. Mr. Malone showed himself a square shooter; he knew I was mixed up with you folks and made me marshal to show that he never plays politics."

She stared at him with lips tightly compressed and fire in her eyes. "Of all the things I ever heard." she exploded at last, "that's absolutely the limit! Bill, why did you do it?"

"Got to work for my protection," he said solemnly. "You know—that orphan asylum job. G'night."

BILL BORDEN closed the door and went up-the street, leaving Molly more puzzled than ever. He was chuckling; he loved to stir her, see the fire in her eyes, hear her sharp retorts. He was flint and she was steel and the sparks never failed to fly.

He heard the commotion before the Gospel tent while he was still half a block away. There was a kerosene flare before the entrance and beneath it he could discern half a dozen or more grouped figures. From their midst came a raucous cry, "Hur-ry, hur-ry, hur-ry! Put your money on the table and pick the shell with the pea beneath it. I pay you two to one if you can do it. It's easy—easy. Step up, gents, and try your luck."

A shell artist had set his table up before the entrance, and the six men gathered before the layout were Malone roughs. Bill frowned and quickened his pace. It was certain that the Reverend Rutherford could conduct no services with this disturbance so near. As he rounded the front corner of the tent Rutherford came out. He strode to where the shell artist stood and put a hand on his shoulder.

The man wheeled. He was a stocky fellow with a red face and a beaver hat. He said, "Want to try your luck, Parson? Step right around to the front and lay the collection on the table. Double your money in two seconds."

Rutherford's deep voice replied, "My friend, you mustn't do this. You are interfering with our worship of the Lord. You will have to go elsewhere."

"Oh, yeah? This is a free country, Parson, and this here lot is free. I got as much right on it as you have." He turned his back and once more launched into his spiel.

Bill saw Rutherford's big hands clench at his sides and saw the flame which leaped into his eyes. The parson controlled himself with an effort and once more appealed to the man. "I tell you this must stop. At once."

A big rough among the six who faced the table stepped forward, hitched his gun belt and said, "Aw, go roll yore hoop, Parson. I got a buck here that says I can pick out the li'l pellet."

He slapped a silver dollar on the table and the dealer instantly put two dollars beside it. He manipulated the three shells deftly, let them come to rest, and the big man picked up one of them; there was nothing under it. The dealer picked up the money, saying, "The hand is quicker than the eye. Try it again, friend. It's easy, once you get the hang of it."

Rutherford let the tautness go out of his frame; his shoulders sagged and his head bowed. He was strong enough to break the gambler in two, but Rutherford was a man of peace. Bill stepped around the tent and saw Nancy standing in the entrance. Her blue eyes were fixed on her father and there was sympathy and pain in them; she turned her head and saw Bill, and her face brightened. She came swiftly to him. "Bill, is there nothing you can do to stop this? It's deliberate, of course. They're trying to break up our meeting."

Bill nodded and stepped up to the gambler. The man's spiel stopped abruptly as Bill's hand fell on his shoulder. Bill flashed his badge and the man stared. Bill said, "The old shell game and six suckers to take the bait. Like to see why that little pill is so hard to catch, boys?"

He brushed the man aside and stepped up to the table. The fellow grabbed his arm and Bill turned a cold pair of eyes on him. "Keep your fingers off me or I'll slap your ears around to the back of your head."

He turned the other two shells over. There was no pea on the table.

"Yes," Borden said, "it's easy. All this gent's got to do is run the shell with the pea under it over this place." He pressed on a foot pedal under the table and a small plug was withdrawn, leaving a hole in the table. "The pea drops through the hole, runs down a little chute to a cup. Plumb easy."

The big man stood scowling at him. "We like it," he growled. "You run along and help the parson roll his hoop. Go on, pilgrim; get started."

His hand dropped to his gun in what would have been a remarkably fast draw. He didn't even get the gun clear; Bill's swivel-holster tipped up and the big man saw the half inch muzzle of the Colt gaping at him. He took his hand off his gun as though the butt had suddenly turned red hot. His face was a brick red. "Gun-artist, huh? Well, you won't get away with it. Monk made you marshal; he can unmake you just as quick."

"One of my duties," drawled Bill, "is to protect you poor, innocent, little boys. Mr. Rutherford, will you kindly collect the hardware?"

He spoke over his shoulder. Rutherford stared at him for a moment, then went around the table. The muzzle of Bill's Colt still yawned at the big man; Bill said, "Unbuckle your belt and pass it over to the preacher."

"Danged if I will!"

Borden thrust out his chin and looked as tough as possible; a double click sounded as he drew back the hammer of the Colt. "I said hand over that belt!"

The big man unfastened the belt, his hands trembling with rage. Rutherford took it and turned to look at Bill questioningly. "Get the others, too," Borden said.

Each man in turn unbuckled his belt and handed it to the preacher.

WHEN THEY were disarmed, Bill said, "Now we're going inside and listen to a good sermon. Follow Reverend Rutherford into the tent. When the services are over, you'll get your guns back. Start moving."

Rutherford's face broke into a smile and his eyes lighted. Bill couldn't see Nancy, but he could almost feel her approval. The big man glared, but Bill glared harder. Bill said, "You're going in, dead or alive; if it's dead, we'll listen to your funeral oration."

The big man turned and stepped into the tent after Rutherford. The others followed sheepishly. Bill brought up in the rear and Nancy fell in beside him and took his arm. Her blue eyes were sparkling and her lips were curved in a warm smile.

There were two dozen or so people in the tent, mostly women, and they stared roundeyed at the procession.

Bill said softly, "Right up to the front, boys, and don't crowd. And take off your hats."

All of them removed their hats except the big man. They filed around the end of the front bench and seated themselves stiffly, uncomfortably. Nancy went up to the organ and Rutherford mounted the little dais and laid the belts on the floor beside him. Bill sat down in the second row immediately behind the big man. He reached out and took the fellow's hat from his head.

Nancy played the opening bars of "Just As I Am" and the congregation sang.

Reverend Rutherford preached. He told the story of the prodigal son; he told it in simple words, forcefully, and in spite of themselves the men in front of Bill were interested. All but the big fellow. He sat straight and frowning and belligerent. When Rutherford said, "Let us pray," all but the big man knelt at once. Bill drew his Colt and nudged him persuasively in the back; the big man knelt, too.

They sang again. It was "How Firm a Foundation" and Bill was surprised when several of his reluctant worshippers joined in. When Rutherford asked the blessing of the Lord upon them, they stood with bowed heads. All but the big man. He stood, because the gun prodded him again, but he didn't bow his head. When the benediction had been pronounced Rutherford came down to them, smiling, and shook their hands. All but the big man; he stuck his hands in his pockets and glared.

"I'm glad you men were with us," said Rutherford. "I wish you'd come again. We're just peaceful folk who ask no more than to worship our Lord in peace and quiet. Get your weapons and go your ways with my blessing."

They wished him goodnight, sheepishly, got their guns and tiptoed from the tent. Bill stood to one side watching the big man; he snatched up his gunbelt, buckled it in place, then slouched over to Bill for his hat, slapped it on his head and said, "You ain't seen the end of this. I was a friend of Biff Bang and I don't like the way you look or talk or walk or anything about you. Next time you see me, start shootin'."

He stamped down the aisle, thrusting aside the people who stood staring. Rutherford had gone to the entrance to wish his congregation good night; Nancy stood by Bill and her hand was on his arm.

He sighed. "I get into the awfullest messes, don't I, Nancy?"

Her eyes were shining. "I think you were splendid, Bill; some of those men were repentant; I could see it in their faces."

"They'll get over it with the first shot of liquor."

"Maybe. But if just one of them would really repent, there would be rejoicing in Heaven."

"There's one sinner in that bunch that there won't be any rejoicing over; and if he don't change his ways mighty sudden, he'll be standing before Saint Peter mighty soon. You heard what he told me."

"Yes. Be careful, Bill; but don't shoot him. It just isn't right."

"Not even to save my life? Nancy, why are you so set on that? You're an intelligent girl; I just can't picture you as a fanatic."

She didn't look at him; she was looking towards the tent entrance and her voice was very low when she spoke. "There was a boy once. He was young, happy-go-lucky, with curly brown hair and eyes that were always laughing. But he learned to use a gun and he got to believe that he—he just couldn't miss." She paused and Bill saw tears trembling on her lashes. "He—had a quarrel—with a man who said something nasty about me. He—well—he—"

She stopped. The tears were running down her cheeks now, and her fingers dug into Bill's arm.

He laid a gentle hand on her shoulder, patted her as he would a little child. "I understand, Nancy; I'm sorry. And I'll try to remember. Good night."

He went out into the cool night. There was something in his throat that he couldn't swallow.

✒ 8 ✒

Catastrophe

AT HIS cabin, Borden got out the wanted notices and refreshed his memory with the contents of one of them. There was no mistake about it; both picture and description fitted. The big man who had told him to start shooting on sight was Cherokee Smith, who had led a band of outlaws in a train holdup and had shot the express messenger. There was a reward of $1,000 for him, dead or alive.

Bill put the notices away and went down town again. He moved about the streets, keeping a sharp lookout for Cherokee, but didn't go into the *Frontier*. He wasn't afraid of Cherokee, but his promise to Nancy would be a handicap if they should meet. Bill would have to shoot to disable, and Cherokee would doubtless shoot to kill.

He went into the *Double Eagle*, saw Wes Peters at the bar and passed him without speaking. The councilman, Frank Cade, was dealing faro at one of the tables; it occurred to Bill that here might be the source of Monk Malone's information. Fred Sivart was in on the secrets of the Cleanup Party, and Cade worked for Sivart, perhaps Sivart had inadvertantly revealed the name of the Cleanup Party's candidate to Cade.

Borden went out again. Noise from the *Frontier* came rolling across the street in continuous waves, but he did not enter. The offer of free drinks had drawn fully two dozen miners into the place; they could take care of themselves and they could tear the joint down for all Bill cared.

He found the *Lucky Tiger* and went in. It was as dirty as was Ed Dillon, its owner, and there was almost as much noise here as in the *Frontier*. The occupants were mostly roughs, probably crowded out of the

Frontier by miners. Girls kept going and coming through a doorway which led to another part of the building, and Bill guessed that Dillon's business was not confined to the sale of beer and whiskey; he took a look around and went out.

The combination marshal's office and jail was next door to the *Lucky Tiger;* Bill unlocked the door, went inside, and lighted a lamp which stood on the battered desk. Besides the desk there was a cot, several straightbacked chairs, a gun rack holding an assortment of weapons, and a brass spittoon. In the top desk drawer was a large key which Bill supposed fitted the cell doors, several pairs of handcuffs and their keys, and a plentiful supply of ammunition. The other drawers were crammed with accumulated wanted notices.

Bill opened a door at the back of the room and, carrying the lamp, went into a dark corridor. There were two cells on each side of the passageway and a back door which was bolted on the inside. He put out the light, locked up and continued his tour of the town.

There were a dozen saloons, all filled. Most of them carried gambling layouts and there were quite a few girls. Bill had never seen such a choice collection of toughs in one town; his conviction grew that the Cleanup Party could never outvote the opposition.

On his way back he entered the passageway between the *Frontier* and the barber shop and looked through a side window; he spotted Cherokee Smith talking with Smoke Rafferty near the doorway to Malone's office. If it hadn't been for his promise to Nancy Borden, he would have walked in and settled their quarrel then and there. Sooner or later there would be a showdown and Bill preferred it sooner; but he had given his word to Nancy.

It was only ten o'clock but he decided to call it a day. The hell with Calder; let the roughs and the cowboys and miners tear it apart and fight over the scraps. He went home and to bed.

SUNDAY again and Borden slept late. There was never anything doing on Sunday mornings. Bill fed himself and his horse, sat for a while studying the wanted notices; he identified fully half a dozen criminals and filed their names and descriptions away in his mind. At ten o'clock he walked down to the *Frontier* and went inside. There was a single bartender and a swamper present and nobody else. The barman said to Bill, "Monk wants to see you. He's inside."

Bill wondered if Monk lived in that one room. He rapped on the door and went in. Where you been keepin' yoreself?"

"I've been around." Bill straddled a chair. "What's on your mind?"

"You! What the blazes you mean by pullin' that stunt at the tent? You wasn't hired to convert the heathen."

"I busted up that shell game because the boys were being rooked."

Monk's scowl became blacker. "You ain't *that* dumb; you know why that feller was planted there."

"Sure I do, but I figured it was a poor play. There was a bunch of women in the tent. You can scare men away from the polls but stuff like that only makes women mad. I'll bet every lady in that tent'll march her husband, or her son or brother, to the polls and make 'em vote for the Cleanup Party, now even if she has to use a club. You're not as smart as I thought you were, Monk."

Malone glared at him and again Bill was impressed at the man's apparent helplessness. He didn't know how to answer; he must have ordered the disturbance, yet he had no logical reason to justify it. He wet his thick lips and cleared his throat; the belligerence went out of him.

"Mebbe it wasn't so smart at that," he conceded. "But you shore got yourself in Dutch by doin' what you did. Cherokee's gunnin' for you." A malicious glint came into his eyes. "Mebbe that's why nobody could find you last night."

"Maybe. I never shoot more than one man a day. Biff was my victim yesterday. I'll put Cherokee at the top of my list if you want me to; where does he hang out?"

"Shack back of the livery corral. Three other fellers with him. If you want to die suddenlike, try bustin' in on them."

Bill let that pass. "Anything else you want to see me about?"

"Reckon not. Keep yore ears open; the Cleanup outfit'll make a lot of what you done last night and might get confidential. And after this make sure about any setup you run into before you go bustin' in."

Bill left and walked up the street to the end of town. Services in the Gospel tent were over and people were coming out; this being Sunday there was quite a crowd. Bill was standing on the sidewalk, watching, when Molly and Fred Sivart came out; she saw him and left Sivart to hurry towards him. Her dark eyes sparkled and her smile made dimples in her cheeks. "Bill, it seems I'm always apologizing to you. I'm sorry that I accused you of going over to the other side. Nancy told me about the six sinners you herded to the altar. It was marvelous. And what a story it'll make! I'm going to write it up for Thursday's paper; I think the Governor will enjoy reading about it."

Fred Sivart joined them, spoke to Bill and smiled—but the smile did not reach his eyes. Bill thought, *The sonofagun's jealous, and I don't blame him.*

Sivart said, "That was nice work last night, Bill. Maybe the Cleanup Party should arm and march all of Malone's men to the meetings. Rutherford might be able to talk a little brotherly love into their souls."

"I'm getting a lot of credit I don't deserve," Bill told them, "I did it as a joke; I thought it would be funny to make them listen. They turned the joke on me by liking it. All except Cherokee Smith; listening to a sermon was a humiliating experience for him."

"I hear he's gunning for you."

"So he was kind enough to inform me."

Quick alarm came into Molly's face and she put her hand on Bill's sleeve. "Bill be careful! He's a desperate and dangerous man."

Borden grinned. "I outdrew him last night; I can do it again."

Sivart said shortly. "Come on, Molly; we'll have to hurry if we want to take a gallop before dinner. So long, Bill. Be good."

He dragged Molly away and Bill's eyes followed them down the street. They made a handsome couple, Sivart's five foot-eleven just the right height for Molly's five foot-four.

THE DAY passed uneventfully. Bill made no effort to evade Cherokee Smith, leaving their encounter to fate; but he didn't meet the big man. He saw Wes Peters in the *Double Eagle* that night but didn't speak to him.

Monday came and went, a dull, uninteresting day. The free drink sign disappeared from the *Frontier's* wall, and miners nursed a bad hangover. No sign of Cherokee Smith, who was probably nursing one also in the shack behind the livery corral.

Tuesday likewise came and went. Hangovers were gone and the town resumed its normal activities. Bill made his rounds and dropped in to see the justice of the peace, Judge Higby. He was a thin little man with a sour face and he complained because of the lack of arrests. Bill told him he'd make up for lost time later on. In the evening he stood outside the Gospel tent more, it must be confessed, to listen to Nancy's sweet voice than to her father's sermon. Molly was busy in the *Clarion* office and he did not disturb her, chiefly because he could think of nothing to make the sparks fly. He saw Cherokee twice, but the man must have seen him first for Cherokee disappeared quickly, each time; that was perplexing since he had seemed quite anxious for a meeting. Either his ardor had cooled or he was waiting until chance favored him; Bill decided that it was the latter.

Tom Harrigan did not come to town and Bill hoped that his supporters had convinced him that discretion is the better part of valor. On the other hand, Tom had had a severe scare and probably a more severe hangover.

Wednesday gave promise of no more excitement than the preceding three days, but when things started that evening....It was after supper and Bill was passing the *Clarion* office on his way down town when Molly saw him and beckoned him to come in. Her father was working on the press, preparing for the run of the paper which would come out the next morning. She slapped the proof of an editorial before him and told him to read it. Her eyes were shining and her color was high.

Bill read it, a blistering condemnation of Malone and his conduct of town affairs. It pulled no punches, accusing Monk openly of harboring criminals for a price, of misappropriating funds and condoning crime. It accused him of planning John Turner's death and stated that Tom Harrigan had been marked as a victim but had been saved by some flaw in the plan.

Bill grinned and nodded his approval. "You finally got the old pick and shovel working; that ought to wake them up. If Monk wins the election there should be an investigation. And he will win it."

"I'm betting the *Clarion* that he won't!"

"And I'm betting a lifetime of service that he will."

"You'll live to regret it. I'll put you to washing dishes and polishing boots and cleaning type and making beds."

"That settles it; I'm voting for Monk. Two or three times if I can work it."

There was an article on the outrage at the Gospel tent and the punishment meted out by the town marshal, "*who,*" the article read, "*seems to have some respect for the Lord remaining in him even if he was appointed by Malone.*"

"Wow!" cried Bill.

"I wrote that!" crowed Molly.

As if he couldn't have guessed!

BORDEN kept his eyes open on the way down the street, looking for Cherokee Smith; this eternal vigilance was wearying and he determined to end it. His course of action

was planned: he would shoot Cherokee in the leg and take a chance of the shock and paralyzing weakness spoiling the man's aim. A man seldom shoots well while trying to stand on a broken leg. But Bill would have to have light for such fast and accurate shooting, so he went into the *Frontier.*

Cherokee wasn't there, Bill went up to the bar, standing at its end where he could watch the door, and started drinking beer.

The outbreak came from the direction of the jail; a sudden fusillade of shots and a chorus of wild yells. Bill went out on the run and turned left; The fracas was at Ed Dillon's *Lucky Tiger.* Men were pouring through the doorway, turning to shoot into the place when they reached the sidewalk. Inside, a loud voice was shouting, "I'm a sonofa gun from Sundown and can lick any six men in this lousy town! Bring on yore gunslingin' marshal and watch me polish him off!"

Bill obliged, leaped through the swinging doors, his Colt in hand. The back bar mirror was splintered and there was broken glass on the floor; the rear light had been shot out and was weeping oil on the sawdust. Only one man was in sight— at the back of the room; a big rough called Big Bob Belcher, wanted for stage robbery and murder.

If the man was drunk, his reactions had not been slowed; even as Bill burst into the room he leaped for the back door, not even loosing a shot in Bill's direction. He yanked open the door and jumped into the dark alley and Bill sprinted in pursuit; it was time, he thought, that Judge Higby collect a fine.

He halted by the piano which stood just to the left of the doorway, not foolish enough to bound into a dark alley with a wild man waiting for him there. He leaped to the right of the doorway and peered out into the blackness, saw nothing and jumped to the left side to look out an another angle. He was backed against the piano and some instinct caused him to turn his head. He was just in time to see the scowling, intent face of

Cherokee Smith over the top of the piano; Cherokee's gun barrel came down in a smashing blow and Bill sank to the floor.

He was not completely out; by the time he recovered his strength he was buried under a pile of human bodies. The pile untangled and they yanked him to his feet. Every one of them had a bandana mask over his face. Bill's gun was gone and half a dozen hands clutched his arms. When he was on his feet, another half dozen hands snatched his legs from under him and he was borne out into the alley.

The rear door of the jail was open; they carried him in and tossed him into a cell. The door slammed and a key grated, then the whole crowd melted into the alley and he was alone with his rage.

He shouted and got no answer; he staggered to the door and shook the bars angrily but also futilely. He climbed up on the cot and shouted through the small barred window and still got no answer. At last, shaking with rage and frustration, he sat down on the cot and tried to compose himself.

Almost instantly he was on his feet again. From far up the street came a new outburst—shots and shouts and above them the sound of metal striking metal. The strokes were rhythmic and punctuated by minor crashes.

He heard boots thud on the board sidewalk; men were running up the street, drawn by the uproar. He sprang on the cot and yelled some more, but his voice only blended with the ones in the distance. He kept yelling until he was hoarse.

The sounds died away and silence fell. An ominous silence. He tried to yell again but the best he could do sounded like a croak. He got down and paced about the cell, trying the bars again even while he realized the futility of it. The marshal was securely locked in his own jail while the devil danced on the devil's doorstep.

Then he heard the pound of boots behind the jail and saw against the lighter blackness beyond the open door a man come bounding into the jail. The man called, "Bill!" his voice sharp with anxiety.

"That you, Wes? Get me out of here; key's in the top desk drawer."

Wes ran through to the office, thumbing a match as he did so. He was back in a few seconds and the key grated in the lock. Bill pushed open the door and leaped out. "What happened?"

"Plenty! A whole crowd of roughs, masked with bandanas, busted into the *Clarion* office. They hustled Sexton and Molly out into the street, then gathered up all the papers and every scrap of proof and burned them in the alley; they busted the press into a thousand pieces with axes, and scattered the type all over creation. They wrecked the place completely; the *Clarion* is done as a newspaper."

Bill leaned against the cell bars and started rolling a cigarette. No use to rush around and get all hot and bothered now. The damage was done and could not be repaired. All cleverly planned and executed, his imprisonment—the ruckus at the *Lucky Tiger* which brought it about—designed to place him in a ridiculous light. The Cleanup Party would believe him a part of the plot, his absence deliberate.

And the editorial which would have brought an investigation to Calder would never be read by the Governor. The feather duster had been discarded too late.

∫ 9 ∫

Behind The Bars

THE TOWN was calming down again and Borden passed men on their way back from the scene of the excitement. In the patches of light where he was recognized, t h e y eyed him furtively and knowingly; his failure to show up when needed was in accordance with the best traditions of a Malone marshal.

Bill hid his red rage beneath an imperturbable expression and went on up to the *Clarion* office. People stood on the sidewalk in front of the place staring curiously and whispering among themselves. The plate glass window had been shattered and the door battered down; type was scattered all over the street. The interior was a wreck, the cast iron wheels and frame of the press broken, the job press a mass of junk, the chairs and desk smashed and hacked. Neither Sexton nor Molly were there.

Bill smouldered under more knowing glances and went to the Sexton home. There was a light inside and when he rapped on the door Molly answered his knock; she gave him one hot look and tried to shut the door in his face, but he put a shoulder between door and frame and forced his way inside.

"You can't do that to me," he told her grimly. "I came to explain and you're going to listen."

"To more lies! I wouldn't believe you now if you swore to your story on a pile of Bibles. You've been working with Malone the whole time; it was you who kept him informed of our plans."

"How about the Gospel tent fire and the suxgun religion? I thought you had stopped doubting me."

"I was a fool. Not for doubting you, for letting you talk me out of it. That stunt at the tent last Saturday night was to get you back into my confidence. You put out the fire because you thought Nancy Rutherford was trapped; you find your amusement in burning orphaned children, not beautiful girls."

"You're as cuckoo as a clock," he told her shortly.

"I was. I'm not any more; I'm cured. Tonight we needed you desperately. You were seen about town just a short time before; if you were with us you would have been on the job. You weren't."

"That's what I want to explain."

"I don't want any explanations. You can never talk me out of my opinion of you. Now go."

"Molly, clamp down the lid for a minute and let me tell you what happened."

"Tell it to the hall; I'm going to bed." She turned and ran up the stairs, and Bill, after a moment, sighed and went out, closing the door behind him.

He went on up the street. The Gospel tent was dark but the little tent behind it where the Rutherfords lived had a light in it. He rapped on the tent pole and presently the flap was flung back and he was looking at Nancy.

She said, "Oh, it's you, Bill."

"Your father inside?"

"No; he's at the Sexton's." She came out and let the flap fall behind her. "Could you talk to me, Bill?"

"You bet I could. I tried to talk to Molly but she ran out on me; I guess she hates me and I can't say that I blame her. But she could have listened to what I had to say."

"Molly's quick-tempered and given to snap judgment. Often she's wrong, and when she realizes she is, she's quick to admit it. Tell me about it, Bill."

BILL TOOK Nancy's hand and led her over to the woodpile. She sat down on the saw horse and he squatted on his heels beside her. He told her just what had happened and offered the bump on his head in evidence.

"Of course," he finished bitterly, "I could have batted myself on the skull to make it look good. After they tricked me I might have if Cherokee Smith hadn't beat me to it."

Her fingers on the sore spot were caressing. "Poor Bill! I believe you, of course; I always have and always will. You must forgive Molly; she's all broken up over the loss of the plant."

"I've forgiven her already. That's the trouble; I couldn't stay mad at her if I wanted to. The question is, will she forgive me?"

"Time is the great healer, Bill."

"Well, it better start healing. And talking about time, that election is creeping up on us. The first Tuesday falls on the first of the month. This is the nineteenth; that leaves eleven days. And Monk Malone is getting hold of our secrets as fast as we hatch them. He must have known of the editorial Sexton was going to print and send to the Governor. The question is, who is the informer?"

"Bill, I can't even guess. But we haven't been as careful as we might. We have people who believe in our cause and are entitled to know our secrets. We talk to them, or give them a hint. Somebody might easily overhear."

"That's the best guess," he agreed. "Frank Cade, one of Malone's councilmen, works in the *Double Eagle*. Wes and the cowboys and miners go there and they naturally talk among themselves. Cade might make it his business to overhear, or he might have friends who hang around for that purpose. He could pass the news on to Monk at one of the council meetings. Monk may even have made him a councilman just to have a spy in our camp."

Nancy sighed. "It's all very confusing, isn't it? But we'll win, Bill; I'm sure of it. The right must triumph."

He left her feeling quite a bit better, though he was even still convinced that right would run a poor second to might in the election to come. He lay awake for a long time that night, planning his campaign.

Thursday and Friday passed without event. Bill kept looking for Cherokee and not finding him. He had a new incentive to spur him, and Cherokee, knowing that Bill had recognized him, had an even greater reason for remaining in hiding.

At noon on Saturday the free drink to miners sign was again over the front of the *Frontier*. Just before supper time Monk called Bill into his office; he was behind his desk as usual.

Malone said, "Jest wanted to tip you off that they's a play comin' up tonight that you ain't in on. Why don't you run up to the Gospel tent and get you some religion?"

"Is that an order?"

"That's an order. Better for you and, mebbe, better for us."

Bill went out trying to guess what the play was to be. Smoke Rafferty was at the end of the bar within two jumps of Monk's door and Bill slipped in beside him and ordered a beer.

"Hear there's something on for tonight," he said casually."

"Did you?" answered Smoke shortly. "Maybe you also heard that you ain't in on it."

"That's right. I'm to go to the Gospel tent and absorb religion. I guess you'll handle it, won't you?"

"Keep on guessin'."

That was all he could get out of Rafferty. Borden moved around the room listening to conversation in the hope of picking up some clue, but if the thing was known it was a carefully guarded secret. He went to a restaurant for supper, still mulling over it. He came back down the street and went into the *Double Eagle;* Tom Harrigan was there and, as on the last occasion, kept glancing across the street and mentally tasting the free liquor being handed out. Bill was immediately seized with a hunch as to what Malone's play was to be.

He was in a quandary. No chance now to get Molly or Nancy to work on Tom, and Harrigan would not listen to him in spite of his close call the preceding Saturday night. It was doubtful if he would listen any more readily to Wes Peters, who was hanging around. Bill glanced about him.

THE CROWD was slim, for it was still early and the miners were across the street. Frank Cade sat at the faro table practicing sleight-of-hand with the cards; Fred Sivart leaned against the end of the bar smoking a long thin cigar. Bill went down and took a place beside him.

He said in a low voice, "Tom Harrigan's going to cross over to the *Frontier* pretty soon, and I got a tip that there's some kind of play being engineered. Can you talk him out of going over?"

"I don't know," said Sivart in the same low voice. "He's stubborn, but I can try. What do you suggest?"

"Tell him they're planning to get him. Persuade him to go with you to jail. Don't let anybody see you and go in the back way. I'll go down ahead of you and open up. Take a quart of liquor along to keep him company. I'll lock him in a cell; nobody'll think of looking for him there."

"Good idea—if it works. Suppose he refuses to go?"

"Slip him a drink that'll knock him cold and we'll carry him down. I tell you, Fred, they're out to get him."

A voice behind them said, "Pardon me, gentlemen."

Bill swung around and saw Frank Cade standing at his elbow. Cade was looking at Sivart.

"I'm about out of cards, Fred. Got some fresh ones in the office?"

"Sure. I'll get them for you. See you later, Bill."

They went away leaving Bill frowning. How long had Cade been standing behind them and how much had he heard? Impossible to tell. There was only one thing to do; Borden moved down the bar to where Wes was standing and bought the cowman a drink. While the barman was getting his change, Bill said, "Stick right in here and keep your eye on Frank Cade. Notice if he goes out or talks with anybody who leaves right afterward. See if he slips anybody a note. This is your chance to help, Wes."

Wes said, "Keno," and Bill moved away.

Sivart and Cade came out of the office and Fred went up to where Tom Harrigan stood, still stretching his neck towards the *Frontier*. Fred said something to Tom and they went into Fred's office together. Presently Sivart came out and nodded slightly in Bill's direction. Bill went out immediately.

He walked to his office, unlocked the door and went in. He got the cell key from the desk and, still in darkness, went down the cell corridor to the back door. He unbolted this, went outside, and stood in the shadows. Within five minutes he heard cautious footsteps and the shadowy forms of two men came into sight. One of them said in a low voice, "You there, Bill?" and he recognized the voice as belonging to Fred Sivart.

He said, "Yes," and led the way into the building.

Harrigan protested. "I don't like this a danged bit, Fred. I'm not runnin' from any man alive."

"You're not running, Tom," Sivard said soothingly. "This is simply a precaution that you owe the Cleanup Party. Once you're mayor, you can go where you please and tell the whole crowd where to head in. I brought along a quart for you, and if you want more one of us'll be seeing you later."

Still grumbling, Harrigan went into a cell, Bill locked the door after him, promised to drop in later, and, after bolting the rear door, went out the front way with Sivart. He locked this door also and they separated at once.

He stopped in at the *Frontier*, saw Smoke Rafferty still standing at the end of the bar, and went out again. He crossed to the *Double Eagle*; Frank Cade was dealing faro. Borden rolled a cigarette, felt in his pockets, then asked Wes if he had a match. Under cover of lighting up, he whispered, "Anything doing?"

"Not a thing. Didn't go out, didn't slip any note. Talked to a couple fellers and one of 'em went out. I know him, and he's all right."

"Stick around and keep watching. I'm going up the street."

BILL WENT to the Gospel tent, entered it and sat down at the back. He wanted to be downtown where he could keep his finger on the pulse of things, but he had to play the game Malone's way in order to avoid suspicion. He was uneasy, and a hunch kept telling him everything was not right. He thought that possibly he had guessed wrong and that somebody other than Harrigan was in danger, might even then be lying with Rafferty lead in him. As soon as Rutherford pronounced the benediction he hurried out and went to the *Frontier*.

Everything was as it had been except that noise and drunkenness had multiplied. Smoke Rafferty still stood at the bar. His uneasiness persisting, Bill crossed to the *Double Eagle*;

Wes reported that Frank Cade had not left the room or handed out a note. He had spoken to lots of men and some of them had afterward gone out, but Wes couldn't possibly check their destinations and watch Cade at the same time.

Fred Sivart came over to them. He had a bottle wrapped in newspaper.

"Better take this down to our friend," he said. "Would have delivered it myself but I forgot to get the key from you."

Bill took the package and went out. He walked to the office, unlocked the door and went inside. It was very still. He got the cell key and went down the dark corridor. "Tom!" he called softly; then, when he got no answer, repeated sharply, "Tom!"

Still no answer. He thumbed a match into flame and held it up. Tom was lying on his back just inside the bars. He hadn't passed out, for his eyes were open and he was staring fixedly at the ceiling. His coat had fallen open and there was a dark stain on his flannel shirt.

And from the middle of that stain protruded the handle of a knife.

∫ 10 ∫

Roundup Time

ILL Borden swore softly, unlocked the cell door, and went in; he knelt by the body in the darkness and felt for some sign of life, knowing as he did so that he would find none. He sat there on his heels, considering. He and Fred Sivart alone knew that Tom had been locked in the cell. Unless Sivart and Tom had been seen on their way here. Unless Frank Cade had heard Bill and Fred talking and had managed to get word to Malone. Those two unlesses bothered him.

The keys. Malone in all probability had a key to the front door; the cell key was in the top desk drawer, though Bill doubted that it had been used. All the murderer had to do was to slip into the dark corridor, whisper, "Tom!" and Harrigan would come close to the bars thinking his visitor was Sivart or Bill. A quick thrust through the bars and it was done. That part was easy to figure.

The killer? Not so easy; it might have been one of a dozen, including Smoke Rafferty and Cherokee Smith. Bill could check on Rafferty, learn if he had left the *Frontier* any time after Borden had gone to the Gospel tent. There was no check on Cherokee, and to check on all the other key Malone men would be next to impossible.

He got up and went into the corridor. There was a lamp hanging from the ceiling and he lighted it. He examined the hallway thoroughly and found that the murderer had neglected to leave behind any clues in the form of discarded handkerchiefs, torn-off buttons, or broken cuff links. He had left nothing, not even tracks; for the floor was of cement.

He went into the office, lighted the desk lamp and searched there. Nothing. He wasn't disappointed; what could he expect to find when all the killer had to do was walk in, stab Tom and go out again?

Bill extinguished both lights and sat down at the desk to study his problem in the darkness. If Sivart and Harrigan had succeeded in reaching the jail undetected, he could conceive only one source through which Monk had received his information. One of the men to whom Frank Cade had spoken had carried the news of Tom's imprisonment to Malone.

As for himself, Bill was in a tough spot. He was the marshal and had the keys to the jail; any hue and cry he might raise over the findings of the body would be interpreted as pure bluff, akin to Biff Bang's charge on the roughs who were raiding the store. The miners, believing Bill guilty, might take the law into their own hands as had Wes Peters and his cowboys in the case of Sam Sneed. It was a rather alarming thought.

Bill muttered, "We'll fix that!" and got up.

He worked swiftly. He went to the

back door and unbolted and opened it, then went into the cell, buttoned Harrigan's coat about him, picked him up carefully and held him cradled in his arms. That was doing it the hard way, but he couldn't sling him over his shoulder without getting blood on himself.

He carried the body out into the dark alley and walked up towards the *Frontier*, pausing every half dozen steps to peer about him and listen. Some distance from the jail and not more than fifty feet from the back door of the *Frontier* he lowered Tom to the ground, arranged him in a sprawling position, unbottoned the coat and opened it. Then he hurried back to the jail.

He bolted the back door, lighted the corridor lamp and examined himself, the corridor and the cell for bloodstains. He found none. Tom had fallen on his back and what blood he had lost had been soaked up by the flannel shirt.

Bill hurried up the street to the *Double Eagle* and entered it; Sivart was not in sight. Borden went to the office, opened the door and went in; Fred was seated at his desk checking over his accounts. He looked up questioningly.

Bill said, "He's gone."

"Gone! Tom?" Sivart was thunderstruck. "What became of him?"

"I don't know. The cell was unlocked and empty. I looked around but didn't find him; and he's not in the *Frontier*."

Sivart was staring at him. "But he can't be gone! I don't understand it. How did he get out with the cell and both doors locked?"

"I don't know. Both doors, front and back, were locked but the cell door wasn't. We better start some of the boys searching for him. I'm worried."

So was Sivart. He said, "I still don't understand."

"I think I do. Malone would have a key to the front door, wouldn't he?"

"Malone? Yes, I suppose so. But Malone didn't know Tom was in the jail. Nobody knew but you and me." His eyes went suddenly hard and cold. "Sure *you* didn't cart him off somewhere?"

"Why should I? I'm the one that suggested putting him there."

"That's what I was thinking."

Bill got it. He said sharply, "Listen, Fred; if I wanted Tom out of the way I could have shot him last week or let Smoke Rafferty shoot him tonight."

"Perhaps you didn't want him killed, maybe you just wanted him out of the way until after election. We couldn't run a missing man for mayor."

"You're as crazy as some other people I know. Come on; let's start looking for him."

THEY WENT into the bar room and Fred called Wes Peters over to them.

"Tom Harrigan can't be found," said Fred. "Bill says he isn't over at the *Frontier*. Get your boys and comb the town; he may be asleep in an alley somewhere and we'd better find him before some of Malone's crowd do."

He's asleep in an alley, all right! thought Bill.

He went out with Sivart and walked along the street with him. They entered every saloon and store they came to, looked about and came out again. They had worked one side of the street and had just come out of Holster's store on the other when Wes came hurrying to them. His face was grim.

"We found him," he reported. "Layin' in an alley on the other side of the *Frontier* with a knife in his chest."

"Dead!" cried Sivart.

"As a mackerel."

"Near the *Frontier*, did you say?"

"Yes."

Sivart turned to Bill, his face distorted with anger. "You did it!" he grated. "You—" He stopped abruptly seeming to pull himself together. "Let's take a look at him," he said.

They walked back into the alley where a small bunch of men had gathered. One of them had a lantern. Sivart knelt and made an examination, then got up and motioned for Bill to take over.

"Ordinary skinning knife," Sivart said. "Dozens of them around."

Bill went through the motions of examining the corpse, then got up and said, "Take him over to Doc Bailey's and tell Doc to fix him up for burial, Wes; get in touch with some of the miners and see if he had any relatives. I'll go down to his cabin and look things over."

He handed Wes the deputy's badge he had in his pocket. "Pin this on you. You're deputized. You and the doc take an inventory of what Tom has in his pockets."

He turned away and Fred Sivart followed him to the street. There Fred halted him. Sivart said, "I guess we'll have to drag this out into the open. We'll have to tell about putting him in the jail and why."

"Guess again," said Bill coldly. "You might just as well accuse me of knifing him."

"I can't help that; I'm coming clean."

"If you say that we locked Tom in the jail, I'll deny it and toss the whole thing smack in your lap. You were the last one seen with Tom while he was alive. He went into the office with you, and you came out without him. Wes saw that and so did others. Somebody might even remember seeing you sneaking through the alley with him, and I was attending the Gospel meeting; better think hard, Fred, before you pop off."

There was a moment of silence, then Sivart said, "All right damn you" and went across the street to the *Double Eagle*.

BORDEN went down to the gulch, found Tom's cabin unlocked and went inside. He found nothing to indicate that Harrigan had any living relatives. There were three buckskin pokes of gold dust hidden under the floor, and Bill appropriated them. Harrigan probably had others more securely hidden.

Bill was mad and getting madder. This thing had gone far enough; they had killed Harrigan in spite of Bill's d e t e r m i n a t i o n that they shouldn't and his dander was up. From here on he'd show Molly Sexton how to use a pick and shovel. And he knew right where to begin.

He walked uptown and found Wes in the *Double Eagle*.

Wes reported, "Usual things in his pockets. No letters. Poke of dust. I made a list and left the stuff with Doc Bailey."

"Good enough. The boys still around?"

"I can round 'em up in a couple minutes."

"Find them and tell them to meet me near the Gospel tent. Have them go up one at a time and on their horses. You be there, too."

He went out and walked to his cabin for his horse. When he dismounted near the Gospel tent Wes and his cowboys were waiting.

Bill said, "We're going after Cherokee Smith and his three buddies. There may be some shooting. You boys with me?"

"You're danged tootin' we are!" said Wes. The others nodded eagerly.

They rode down an alley to the livery corral and spotted the shack where Cherokee and his pals lived. It was lighted. At Bill's command, they dismounted and led their horses, and he disposed them about the place and turned his horse over to Wes.

"If I start shooting, come running," he said tersely.

He moved away before Wes could question, walking quickly and silently towards the shack. He circled it at a safe distance, sizing it up, then moved quietly to a window and looked through the grimy pane. There were four men in the room.

Two of them were in their bunks, reading; a third sat in a chair sewing a patch on a shirt. Cherokee Smith was in a tilted rocker with his feet on a table rolling a cigarette. He was wearing his gun.

Bill reasoned that the doors would be barred, and any tinkering with them would only alarm the occupants. He drew his Colt, made one swift slash at the pane, then thrust the weapon through the hole before the glass had ceased to tinkle.

"Hold it!" he barked. "Hands up, everybody!"

Cherokee was already in action.

With one heave he threw the chair over, did a backward sommersault and came up on his knees with his gun blazing. A bullet nicked Bill's ear and glass bit at his face, and as he ducked sideways another slug kissed his cheek. Because of his promise to Nancy he was taking desperate chances, for he could have killed Cherokee before that second shot.

He fired, and the left arm which supported Cherokee buckled like a matchstick; the man plunged forward on his face. Bill aimed deliberately and fired again, and the gun flew from Cherokee's right hand as the bullet smashed his wrist. Bill heard Wes's yell and the thunder of hoofs.

ONE OF the men in the bunks had rolled to the floor and had the big table between himself and Bill. Bill saw a hand snatch at the gunbelt on a chair by the bunk and snapped a shot at it. The hand was jerked back with great dispatch.

Horses slid to a stop and boots hit the ground. Wes appeared at Bill's side and added the menace of his own .45. Bill said to the man in the chair "Go over and open the front door; and don't make any mistakes."

The man obeyed, and Wes's punchers crowded into the room.

Bill said to Wes, "Have the boys disarm them, tie their hands and herd them out here. Saddle their horses, put them on them and take them to the Gospel tent. I'll meet you there."

Wes had brought his horse and it was standing over hanging rein. Bill mounted and rode to the livery stable. The councilman who looked and smelled like a horse was standing in the rear door beneath a lantern. He recognized Bill and asked, "What's goin' on down there?"

"Just a little personal argument; better stay away until they settle it."

Two roughs came running through the stable and Bill warned them likewise. They hesitated, but there was silence now around the shack and the meddling marshal was right there with them, so they finally turned back. Bill waited five minutes or so, talking with Pete Stacy, then said goodnight in a casual voice and rode to the Gospel tent.

The cowboys and their prisoners were waiting for him. He said, "Out to the ranch. That log stable strong enough to hold 'em over night?"

"You betcha," said Wes.

They had to ride slowly, for Cherokee Smith was in agony. They had fixed up arm and wrist as best they could. It took them two hours to make the trip and the ranch house was dark when they approached it. They put the prisoners in the strong barn, barred the doors and posted two guards. The small windows had two-by-fours nailed across them, Wes having guessed the purpose for which the structure was to be used.

Bill went into the bunkhouse with Wes and the three remaining cowboys; they lighted the hanging lamp and sat down at the table. Bill got out a wanted notice and spread it for them to see. "Cherokee's wanted for train robbery and murder. His companions in the holdup were not described, but I'll make a guess that these three are the ones. In the morning I want you to take them to the county seat and turn them over to the sheriff. Take this notice with you and tell the sheriff to grill them on Harrigan's death and Malone's protection racket. What reward money you collect you can split among you."

Wes said, "My share goes to Miz Turner and the kids."

"Mine too," said the other three in a chorus.

Bill said, "That's swell. An this'll mean four less votes for Malone. Hurry back, for there'll be more shrinkage before we get through. Find me a sheet of paper and an envelope, Wes; I want to write a note to the sheriff."

He wrote swiftly for a few minutes, then folded the paper and sealed it inside the envelope and gave it to Wes. "All this is strictly on the quiet," he told them sternly. "Don't mention what we've done to a soul, unless you have to explain to Mrs. Turner. If you do, swear her to secrecy. We're playing a dangerous game, boys, and we mustn't slip; the whole cleanup of Calder may depend upon your discretion."

"We're tight as clams," said Wes. "But, Bill, it ain't fair that you go without any of this reward money. You better take a cut."

"Well, I will. I reckon about two-thirds would be right." Then, when they stared, he chuckled and added, "But I can't let you fellers get ahead of me; I'm donating my share to Mrs. Turner also."

Wes said, "Bill, you're sure a white man!"

"Thanks, Wes. Everybody won't agree with you."

"Malone, for one," grinned Wes.

Bill observed him thoughtfully. "Malone? I wonder."

∫ 11 ∫

More Shrinkage

IT WAS long after midnight when Bill rode back into Calder, and he went at once to the *Frontier*. The noise which had abated when the stunned miners learned of Harrigan's death had resumed its normal volume, liberal shots of whiskey and music from the two-piece orchestra contributing to the recovery from the shock.

The miners guessed that Harrigan's death had come at the hands of one of Malone's toughs, but his murder did not affect them directly because they were unaware of Harrigan's candidacy. It was a personal matter entirely and just Tom's hard luck that he had come out second best.

Smoke Rafferty, still at the end of the bar, saw Bill enter and jerked his head towards Malone's office. Bill went in. Monk, as usual, was behind his desk and his heavy face wrinkled in a scowl at sight of Bill. "Where in blazes you been?"

Bill sat down and said coldly, "Investigating the murder of Tom Harrigan and taking care of things in general."

"You sure can make yourself hard to find when I want you. What was Harrigan doin' layin' in the alley so near to my place?"

"Well, he wasn't sleeping."

"Who killed him?"

"Why ask me? You ought to know."

"Dang you, feller! You keep a civil tongue in your mouth! If I knowed who killed him I wouldn't waste time askin' you."

Bill was forced to agree that this was true. Monk knew that Harrigan had been slated for death the preceding Saturday night, and Monk knew that Bill knew; there was no reason for evasion between them on this point. An idea that was gradually taking form in his mind grew stronger.

"Only way I can figure," Monk went on, "is that somebody knocked him off for his wad."

"He wasn't knifed for his money. We found a poke of gold on him. We took an inventory of his stuff and left it with Doc Bailey. And I went over to his cabin and found another poke there."

Bill drew a poke of gold dust from his pocket. The other two he had left at the Turner ranch for safekeeping. Monk said, "Hand it over."

"Why?"

"I'm mayor, ain't I?"

"More sinews of war for the organization, huh?"

"What do you think? He ain't got nobody to leave it to."

Bill weighed the gold in his hand. "About three hundred dollars, I should say." He put the poke in his lap, got out a pencil and tore a sheet of paper from a tablet on the desk. He wrote:

Received of Calder's marshal, one poke of gold containing about three hundred dollars, property of Thomas Harrigan, deceased, to be used by the organization.

(Signed)

He pushed it across the desk and said, "Put your John Hancock to that and it's all yours."

Monk read it and pushed it back. "I ain't signin' nothin'. You hand over that poke."

"No tick-ee, no wash-ee. I'm in bad enough as it is; I'm going to take the blame for Tom's death and you know it. He was the Cleanup Party's candidate and I was one of the original seven who knew it. I've got to be in the clear. You sign that or I'll turn the gold over to Rutherford to hold."

Monk stared at him angrily, then drew the paper towards him and re-read it. "What's this 'deceased'? Tom wasn't sick."

"Maybe I spelled it wrong. Maybe it should be 'beceased', meaning that he's ceased to be. Don't matter; just makes it sound better."

Monk scratched 'deceased' out and wrote 'dead' in its place, then scrawled his signature. Bill said, "Much obliged," took the paper and handed over the gold. Monk had missed the significant part of the receipt, the part which acknowledged that the gold was to be used by the organization.

BORDEN went out with his opinion of Malone lower than it had been before. The organization was supposed to be a smart one; either it was greatly overrated or its brains were being supplied by somebody other than Monk. Frank Cade came to Bill's mind.

He hung around town, keeping his eye on the men he had identified from wanted notices. He followed four of them to their homes; two from the *Frontier*, one from the *Lucky Tiger*, and the fourth from a joint called the *Gold Standard*, locating the places where they lived and filing the information in his brain for future reference. It was three o'clock when he turned in.

He awoke the next morning at the usual time, realized that it was Sunday and turned over and went to sleep again. When he awoke again it was nearly nine. He got up, fed his horse and then himself, put on a clean shirt and scarf and walked up to the Gospel tent. He stood near the entrance watching the people who entered. He got some dirty looks from the women and no recognition whatever from the men. Molly passed him between Fred Sivart and her father; they ignored him when he raised his hat, but he saw the angry color in her cheeks and her dark eyes smouldered.

He heard the creak of wheels and turned his head and saw a spring wagon coming up the street. In it was a long wooden box and its driver was Doc Bailey, dressed in a black frock coat and a beaver hat. Four men sat on the box, looking gloomy. They were burying Tom Harrigan in a hurry.

The wagon pulled up outside the tent, the box was unloaded and the four men carried it inside. Bill crossed to the woodpile and sat down on the saw horse. He sat there for an hour smoking and listening to the strains of the melodeon and the deep voice of Reverend Rutherford.

The service ended, the four men came out with the box and pushed it into the wagon, then climbed aboard themselves. Doc Bailey got on the seat, said "Giddup" to the horses and moved slowly down the street. Rutherford and Nancy came out, followed by Sivart and Molly and her father and the rest of the congregation. They moved in a grave procession towards Boothill. Bill rolled another cigarette and composed himself for another hour's wait.

Rutherford and Nancy returned alone; they were about to enter their quarters when Nancy saw Bill. She spoke to her father and the two of them came over towards him. He got up and removed his hat and Rutherford said, "Good morning, Bill. I haven't see you lately. Did you attend the funeral?"

"No. I didn't know Harrigan very well and it would have looked like hypocrisy on my part; they all think I had a hand in his death."

"I don't," said Nancy promptly. "I can't see why people don't realize that you took the job of marshal to help us." .

Her answer startled him. "You believe that, Nancy?"

"Of course. You saved Tom from being shot by Marshal Bang; I'm sure of it. You would have tried to save the *Clarion* too, but Malone had you beaten and locked in jail. And last night when Harrigan was killed, you were in the Gospel tent; I saw you sitting in the back row."

Her faith touched Bill. He said after a moment, "I'd like to tell you what really happened last night."

"We'd like to know, Bill," said Rutherford. "Come into the tent."

He went with them into their living quarters. It was cramped but tidy. Nancy indicated a little curtained-off corner with a faint smile. "My boudoir. Sit down, Bill."

BORDEN told them of his hunch that Harrigan was to be shot and the plan he and Sivart had carried out in an attempt to save Tom; he even told them of his moving the body. "It looked to me as though I was slated to take the blame and I couldn't do that. I want to be free to see this thing through. Mr. Rutherford, what do you know of Frank Cade?"

"Cade? Just that he works for Fred Sivart and is a councilman. Why?"

"I'm trying to spot the leader of this crooked outfit."

"Surely you know it's Malone."

"The more I see and talk with Malone the more I doubt it; I believe somebody is using him for a front, and it looks to me like Frank Cade. This is what I have to go on: First, I saw an arm signal with a handkerchief to Sam Sneed right before Turner was shot; that arm was in a black sleeve and Frank Cade wears a black frock coat. Second, the placard that was nailed on Hollister's store was neatly printed, with all the words spelled correctly; Cade is an educated man and skillful with his hands. Third, as one of Malone's councilmen he is in constant contact with Malone, and his working for Sivart

gives him the chance to learn what the Cleanup Party is doing. Fourth, he's the only person who could possibly have heard Fred and I plan to put Harrigan in the jail. And finally, I just talked with Malone and I believe he's as much in the dark about the killer as I am. Frank Cade was watched, and was seen to talk to any number of men who afterwards left the *Double Eagle*. He could have arranged the murder himself without letting Malone in on it." .

Rutherford and Nancy were watching him intently. After a moment Rutherford said, "It could be, Bill; it could very well be. I must warn Fred about that man."

"Please don't; don't mention what I've told you to anybody. I'm on the inside where I want to be, and things are so tight that I wouldn't even trust my own brother." He smiled and added, "Which should show you how much I think of you two."

"We appreciate your confidence," said Rutherford warmly. "We will say nothing to anybody."

"Thanks. Who are you going to run in Harrigan's place?"

The preacher and his daughter exchanged worried glances. Rutherford said, "I'm sorry, Bill. We'd tell you in a minute but we've passed our word not to. Molly and Leander and Fred insisted that we keep the name a secret until election day. Don't think that we don't trust you; we do."

"Yes, I think you do. It's probably best that I don't know; if anything happens to the new candidate they'll know I wasn't the informer."

They urged Bill to stay to dinner, but he declined, feeling that his presence as a guest might cause them embarrassment should it become known; but he left them with the warm feeling that he had found that rarest of treasures, true friends.

Towards evening things started humming again, with the free drink sign still flaunting itself above the *Frontier* entrance. There was much talk but no trouble of any kind. Bill had found that Calder's outbreaks came at intervals, like tropical storms, with peaceful periods intervening.

He followed four more men to their homes that night, then checked their descriptions against the wanted notices to be sure. The notice describing Al Travis again caught his attention, and once more he studied it. Age, 26. That would fit Frank Cade. Height, 5 feet, 11 inches. Cade again. Weight, 175. A bit on the heavy side, but within ten pounds. Color of hair, blond, Well, hair can be dyed. Color of eyes, blue.

That tore it. Cade's eyes were brown and Bill had never heard of any way to change the color of eyes. No use investigating Cade's chest for a six-inch knife scar. He was tempted to tear up the intriguing notice but didn't.

Wes and the boys were not in town that night, nor did Bill expect them. It would take a day to travel to the county seat and another to return.

WES CAME to town right after supper on Monday night. Bill gave him a signficant look and he followed Bill to the street. They met in an obscure corner of an alley and Wes reported. The sheriff had welcomed them with open arms and their prisoners with open cells. A doctor had worked on Cherokee and he had been grilled. No dice. The other three were identified as Cherokee's companions in the train holdup. The reward would be forwarded to Mrs. Turner. One of the men had admitted paying for protection, but claimed the collector had been Biff Bang.

"He might have collected it," said Bill, "but he didn't keep it. Sheriff say anything about my letter?"

"Looked right pleased and excited. Said he'd do what you asked—whatever that was."

"Like to round up another bunch tonight and collect some more rewards?"

"Does a hoss like oats? The boys are out at the ranch but I can get 'em in a hurry."

"Not too early. Suppose you meet me at the tent around midnight."

It was easy. Two of the men Bill had selected for capture lived together, the other two lived alone; they tackled the pair first. Two of the cowboys were assigned to catch up and saddle the horses; the other three were posted outside to prevent interruption. The door was not locked. Bill and Wes walked into the cabin, yanked the awakened men out of their bunks, lighted a lamp and set it in a corner where it would not show too plainly, and waited while the killers dressed. Bill had brought handcuffs from the jail and these were snapped about their wrists and they were taken outside and turned over to two of the cowboys. They were roped on their horses and sent with the two to the ranch.

At the next house one man caught up and saddled while two watched. Again Wes and Bill walked in and brought out a prisoner. He was roped securely to his horse and sent with two of the cowboys to the ranch for safekeeping.

The third door was locked, but Bill's cautious knock brought the occupant to the door with a whispered, "Who is it?"

"The marshal," said Bill softly. "Monk has a job for you."

The fellow got dressed and walked right into the hands of the receivers.

Wes grinned. "Why didn't we think of this before? Saves trouble."

"We'll improve with practice," Bill told him. "You and your remaining hand take him over. Here are the four notices; three carry rewards and something may have been offered for the fourth by this time. Take 'em to the county seat tomorrow and tell the sheriff to put 'em through the mill. Four of you ought to be enough for the trip; that'll leave two to take care of the ranch chores."

Wes was quite happy about it. "Four more votes lost to Malone. Shucks, Bill, this is fun! If it keeps up, Miz Turner and the kids can give up cow ranchin' and take to snatchin' outlaws. More money in it."

"I reckon," said Bill grimly, "that all the rewards for all the criminals in the world wouldn't make up for John's loss."

"That's right," agreed Wes soberly. "But you sure have done your bit to pay her back."

"I've been hanging around the Gospel tent too much," grinned Bill. "I must be getting religion."

⌇ 12 ⌇

Ambush

 TUESDAY was quiet outwardly; inwardly things were beginning to stew. Borden had hardly gone into the *Frontier* when Smoke Rafferty came from Malone's office and told Bill that Malone wanted to see him. The dandified gunman was tightlipped and bright-eyed and Bill gave him no chance to get behind him. When he entered the office he remained standing until Rafferty, at a signal from Monk, sat down; then he took a chair where he could watch both men.

Monk said abruptly, "Where's Cherokee?"

"I know where I wish he was; it was him that batted me over the head down at the Lucky Tiger."

"I know that; I'm askin' you where he is."

"You'll have to keep on asking. I don't know."

Monk eyed him steadily. "Saturday night Pete Stacy said there was some shootin' down at the shack. Stacy seen you around there. Sunday mornin' Cherokee and his two pals turned up missin'."

"Saturday night," said Bill, "Tom Harrigan was killed; but I didn't kill him,"

"Quit dodgin' and talk."

"All right. I walked into Cherokee's shack on Saturday night, shot all three of them, buried them in a hurry and then exchanged jokes with Stacy."

"Damn you, feller! I warned you about tryin' to make a monkey of me!"

"You're making a monkey of yourself. You told me it was sudden death to try to walk in on those three; have you changed your mind?"

"Maybe you tricked 'em. I'm beginnin' to think you're pretty slick thataway."

"If I had shot Cherokee and his pals I'd be bragging about it, not denying it. You say they've disappeared; what could I have done with them?"

"I dunno; I sure don't. Things are happenin' around here that never happened before, and they didn't start nappenin' until you showed up. I know that Cherokee told you to come shootin' next time you seen him. When he turned up missin' I thought of you right off."

"Are their horses gone?"

"Yeah."

"Looks to me like they cleared out. I hope so. If the other two were like Cherokee I won't miss 'em. That all you wanted with me?"

"Yeah. But I still ain't satisfied. Figger out who killed Harrigan?"

"Sure—one of your bunch. He was the Cleanup Party's candidate."

"I told you I didn't know nothin' about it."

"Maybe somebody did it as a favor to you and is too modest to say so."

"Aw, get the hell outa here!"

Bill backed out and Rafferty got up and followed him. At the bar Rafferty said, "I ain't satisfied either. I got a hunch you're playin' Monk for a sucker. I got another hunch that you put somethin' over on Cherokee. He's another friend of mine; that makes two of my friends you got to account for."

"You start crowding me, Smoke, and I'll account for the best friend you have—yourself."

"You and how many more?" sneered Rafferty.

"After taking care of Cherokee and his two gunslinging pals, do you think I need any help?"

Evidently Rafferty wasn't sure about that, for he said nothing more.

When Bill walked up the street he was surprised to find that new glass had been out in the *Clarion* window, a new door hung, and that the debris had been cleaned up. Furthermore, Molly Sexton was seated at the damaged desk sorting large type from a pile before her. He opened the door and went in and leaned against the desk.

"Is our star reporter still mad, or has her better judgment prevailed?"

She observed him coldly. "No, I'm not mad. I've just decided that since I have nothing to do with other Malone minions I should have nothing to do with you."

"Still think I'm the tale-bearer, huh?"

"More so than ever since Saturday night."

"Which means that Fred told you of our plan to save Harrigan and the way it kicked back in our faces. Did he mention Frank Cade?"

"What has Frank Cade got to do with it?"

"He may have everthing to do with it. He was standing behind us when we talked the thing over; he might have heard. When Harrigan was killed I was up at the Gospel tent. Malone told me to absorb some religion. I think he wanted to get me out of the way but knew he couldn't work the same trick he used the night the *Clarion* was wrecked."

Her dark eyes were wide. "What trick was that?"

"The one I called to tell you about. You didn't want to hear about then; now you do. Talk about a woman changing her mind!"

"You don't have to tell me; I'm not particularly anxious to hear."

"Fine." He straightened. "You'd probably say I was lying any how. Well, as Nancy told me, time is the great healer. Good day, Miss Sexton."

He started for the door and she called, "Bill!" He turned his head and she asked, "Does Nancy know—about that trick?"

"Sure. She's always willing to give a fellow a break. She even saw the bump on my head."

He opened the door and Molly called, "Wait, Bill! What bump?" But he just said, "It's gone now," and went on out. He was chuckling again; tormenting Molly was fun. He crossed the street and stood in a passageway between two buildings, and presently he saw her come out and hurry towards the Gospel tent. He chuckled again and went to the cabin.

THAT NIGHT when Bill was in the *Frontier*, Rafferty slipped up to the bar beside him and said, "Four more of our fellers are gone. Know anything about them?"

"Take their horses?"

"Yes."

"Then why ask me? You're getting as bad as Monk; when I get through with fellows they don't need horses, they need hearses."

"I got a hunch you're fixin' to ride in one of them things yourself!"

Bill said, "It might be fun; I never rode in one before," and went out to roam about the town. Very soon he realized that he was being followed His shadower kept far enough away to avoid being recognized, and Bill pretended to be unaware of his presence; he believed he could shake the fellow whenever he pleased.

Wednesday was uneventful, too, but the same air of tension persisted. Wes showed up in the *Double Eagle* that night, and Bill had a drink with him and designated a meeting place, setting the time for half an hour later. He went out, proceeded to lose the man who still stuck to his trail, and arrived at the meeting place just as Wes appeared.

Wes gave his report. The prisoners had been delivered safely, and had been grilled. Apparently they knew nothing of Harrigan's death. One confessed to paying five hundred dollars for protection, and named Monk Malone. He seemed bitter because Monk had allowed him to be taken.

"Got another bunch ready for us?" asked Wes.

"Not tonight. I'm being shadowed and we mustn't get caught at this.

Monk is worried and Smoke Rafferty's getting the jitters in his trigger finger. If no more men disappear between now and Sunday, they may pull off the trailer. We'll line some up for Sunday night; you can take them to the county seat on Monday and get back in time to vote on Tuesday."

On Thursday morning he ran into Molly. She was distributing printed sheets in places of business and handed him one to read. It consisted of a single paragraph printed in large type on a single sheet of paper. It said:

The Malone machine is responsible for the deaths of John Turner and Tom Harrigan and the wrecking of the CLARION. This is common knowledge. If we want a decent town and an honest administration we must destroy that machine. If you do your duty and vote for the Cleanup Party's candidate for mayor the machine is done. For his own protection our candidate's name will not be announced until election day.

"How'd you get this out?" he asked.

"We found an undamaged frame and collected the type from the street. We set it up, ran an inked roller over the type and printed the sheets one at a time. We're going to follow up with a new sheet every day between now and Tuesday. You're going to owe me that lifetime of service in spite of everything Monk Malone can do."

"You haven't much to lose with the *Clarion* down to one frame, some secondhand type and an ink roller, but the bet's still on."

"If you win, you'll be paid its equivalent in some form," she said proudly; "the Sextons don't welch on their bets. And, Bill—" She hesitated and the pink crept into her cheeks. She went on bravely. "I talked with Nancy. She told me— what you would have told me if I hadn't been too mad to listen, Bill, I—I guess I'm sorry again."

"Forget it," he said cheerfully. "I wouldn't feel natural if you didn't doubt me at least twice a week. Still keeping the name of your candidate a close secret, I see."

She said "Yes" and looked doubtful. He hurried to add, "Don't tell me; you always regret it later."

She shifted the bundle of papers to the other arm and he caught sight of something which for some reason hit him like a blow below the belt. "What's that on your finger?"

"That? An engagement ring."

"I see. I was afraid it was; have you set the date?"

She stared at him for a moment, then composed herself and lowered her eyes. "Not yet. It—it's quite tentative."

BILL'S feet dragged a bit as he went up the street. So she was going to marry Fred Sivart. Well, why not? No reason for him to be bothered, unless it was the thought of not having her to torment any more. A fellow doesn't feel so free to exchange banter with another man's wife. Anyway, it wouldn't have lasted much longer; get this business in Calder over and then for new pastures. He straightened his shoulders and quickened his pace.

He spent Friday counting noses and making guesses. Even the most optimistic of them gave Monk Malone a slight edge in the voting. Very slight. One more good haul of Malone supporters and the balance might tip in favor of the Cleanup Party. He wanted Molly to have the satisfaction of crowing over him and he wanted the Rutherfords to enjoy their moral victory; he visualized the shining face of Nancy when her faith in the right was justified.

The ominous quiet which had prevailed continued into Saturday. The free drink sign went up over the *Frontier* and by the time darkness fell the town was crowded. There was a lot of noise and a few fist fights, but no real disturbance. Bill arrested half a dozen of the fighters and put them in jail after Judge Higby had fined them; it was a mere gesture, but it made the judge happy and helped Bill keep up a front.

The shadower still kept on his trail.

Friday and Saturday had brought out new editions of the abbreviated *Clarion* consisting of pep talks condensed into a paragraph or two; Bill had to concede that they might have some effect on the timid ones.

Sunday morning slid by dully, became an afternoon of gradually increasing tempo, and ran into a night of heated argument and more fist fights. Bill became suddenly very diligent, arresting miners and cowboys right and left. He appeared to be working hard for Malone but wasn't; election was drawing very near and men in jail couldn't get drunk. The less Cleanup Party hangovers on Tuesday, the more votes. Probably as a sign of approval on the part of Monk, the shadower was called off. His absence suited Bill's plans to a T.

Wes was in the *Double Eagle* and Bill found the chance to whisper to him, "Midnight. Same place."

At eleven he started his plan moving. He had selected six men wanted for crimes ranging from horse theft to murder. He moved about the saloons singling them out. To each he said, "Be at Cherokee Smith's shack at twelve. Go alone and wait inside. Some of the other boys will join you there. There's something on tap and Monk don't want us to meet at the *Frontier* because the Cleanup outfit will be watching it. Not a word to anybody."

By eleven forty-five he had notified all six. He got his horse and rode to the Gospel tent and found Wes and his five waiting. He told them of the setup.

"'You boys fan out and keep out of sight. I'll walk in on them and light a lamp. I'll go into a spiel about a raid on the gulch and hold their attention while you close in. Be careful. It's risky, but we got to go it. I couldn't take the chance of telling them to fetch their horses, but Pete Stacy's down at the Frontier and there's nobody around the livery corral. A couple of the boys can hitch a team to a wagon and park it somewhere near the shack. We'll load them into that."

Wes said, "You're the feller that's takin' the risk, walkin' in on that bunch. If they smell a rat it'll be just too bad for you."

"We'll have to play them as they fall, Wes; if it breaks bad, get out of here fast. Now go to your positions. I'll wait five minutes before I go to the shack to give you time to hitch up."

They left, two of them riding directly to the livery corral. When the five minutes had expired, Bill started for the shack.

He tied his horse to a tree a hundred yards from the cabin and went ahead on foot. He did not skulk and he did not pause. Half a dozen pairs of eyes would be watching for him from the shack and he must approach it boldly as though there was no deceit in him. The door was open, but it was so dark inside that he couldn't see a thing. The silence almost shrieked.

He felt the hair at the back of his neck prickle in warning; an uneasy hunch that all was not well seized him; but he couldn't hesitate now. Although his nerves were keyed to their highest pitch and every relaxed muscle was ready to tauten, his voice as he stepped over the sill was casual.

"You fellers all here?"

"You're damned right we are!" came the vicious reply. "Let the lousy son have it, boys!"

THE FELLOW strung it out just a second too long. Already warned by that hunch, the venom in the voice was all the confirmation Bill needed. Before the first sentence was fairly out, Bill crouched and leaped to the left into the blackness of a corner.

It was instinctive, the immediate response of a brain trained to reason swiftly in emergencies. The men would be bunched at the far end of the cabin where they would be safe from their own searching lead, and once out of the doorway Bill would not be visible to them.

A blast like thunder shook the shack and orange flame leaped from the muzzled of sixguns.

He was flat on the floor, his gun out, but he didn't fire. He recalled the location of the furniture as he had seen it through the window the night they had taken Cherokee. Under cover of the shots which continued to pour from guns, he crawled forward along the side wall and found the end of a bunk. He went under it like a lizard, crawled to the upper end and lay quiet.

The firing ceased. There was a moment of silence, then a voice said, "You reckon we got him?"

"How could we miss?" answered another. "Take that lamp in a corner and light it."

A match flamed within five feet of Bill's head, and from beneath the bunk he saw the figure of a crouched outlaw. The man had removed the lamp chimney and was gazing fearfully towards the end of the cabin. Not seeing a sixgun aimed at him, he glanced down and put matchflame to wick.

One of the outlaws said, "Some fellers comin' at a run!"

"They would," said another. "Fetch that lamp out here where we can see."

The man with the lamp moved forward, holding the light at arm's length ahead of him. The whole six edged towards the doorway, following the creeping arc of light, crouched over, guns ready.

Bill slid under the head of the bunk, came around on his knees and leveled his Colt over the bed.

A man said, "He ain't—!" and whirled. He saw Bill and his gun whipped up. Bill shot him clean through the head.

Borden fired again as they wheeled, knocked another man down, snapped a shot at a third, then ducked behind the bunk as answering slugs tore through it. Putting his head and shoulders beneath the bunk, he fired from the side and another man collapsed with a broken leg.

Wes's voice rang out, "Hold it! We got you covered!" and the firing abruptly ceased. Wes cried anxiously, "Bill, you all right?"

Bill crawled out from under the bunk. "All present or accounted for. Quick, boys! The whole town'll be here in a minute. Disarm these birds and get 'em out of here. Two of you carry the one with the broken leg. Don't bother with the two on the floor; they're dead. Make it fast!"

They worked like beavers. Guns and knives were taken from the four living outlaws, their wrists were tied. The three bound prisoners were hustled from the room by the three of the cowboys while the other two carried the wounded man.

Bill said, "Here are the wanted notices for all six. Take 'em to the county seat first thing in the morning. Get back before sundown on Tuesday if you have to kill some horses doing it. The Cleanup Party'll need your votes and I'll need your guns."

He left Wes and headed for the tree where his horse was tied. He mounted, rode a short distance away and sat waiting. He heard the rumble of wheels and saw the wagon heading for the ranch with the team galloping. Wes's cowboys surrounded it. From the direction of Main Street came the sound of shouted questions and pounding boots. Running figures rounded the livery stable and headed for Cherokee's shack.

Bill grinned mirthlessly and reined away. Six more votes lost to Malone!

∫ 13 ∫

Election Day

 MONK Malone was furious. For the first time since he had known him, Bill was getting a good look at the man; Malone had got up from his desk and was stamping up and down the office as he raged.

Standing near the side door was Smoke Rafferty, composed but alert, his mean eyes glinting. Standing against the opposite wall was Bill, equally composed, equally alert, equally glinting of eye. It looked like the showdown.

"You can't deny you done it!" shouted Monk. "One of them fellers was suspicious and come to me before he went to the shack. I told him I never sent no message to meet at Cherokee's, and he said he'd danged well take care of you. And I said go ahead; you'd double-crossed me just one time too often!"

Bill wasn't ready for the showdown yet; election day was the day he had picked. He said, "Sure I gave him that message. Sure I used your name. Think he'd have gone down there if I hadn't? I wanted to talk to them where we wouldn't be overheard. I had an idea."

Bill was careful of his words. Two dead men had been found in the shack; if one of them was the man who had gone to Monk, Malone would not know there had been more than just those two in the party; if the man who had seen him was one of the four prisoners, Monk would know that there were at least three. Malone's next words set him right on this. "I'll say you had an idea! You had the idea you could get them down there and bump both of 'em off."

Bill said, "Listen, Monk, and sit down; no use getting all stirred up. You got your own little graft and I thought I'd have one of my own. I knew both of those hairpins; one is Cole Brent, wanted for murder, and the other is Ed Foley, wanted for horse theft. I was going to talk things over with them and come to some sort of understanding. After all, I'm marshal of Calder; I could make 'em think I'd turn them in if they didn't come across."

Monk regarded him through beady eyes. "How come you knew them?"

"I didn't know them personally, but I saw some wanted notices that fitted them mighty close."

"Yeah? Where'd you see them notices?"

"Down at the jail. The desk drawers are full of 'em."

It sounded logical enough, and

Monk lost some of his belligerence. He sat down heavily, still scowling.

"He's bluffin'," said Rafferty harshly. "Don't let him make a sucker of you, Monk."

"You keep your yap out of this, lapdog," grated Bill. "Monk's got brains; he can think for himself." Borden crossed his fingers mentally as he said it.

"Yeah," agreed Monk. "You stand hitched, Smoke." He turned back to Bill. "If you hadn't been arrestin' Cleanup fellers right and left I'd take your badge and mebbe turn Smoke loose on you. Looked for a while there like you was workin' for the Cleanup outfit; now I ain't so sure. Get out and let me think it over."

Bill said, "You'll figure it out right, Monk; you're smart."

He reached behind him and opened the door, then backed out and closed it. He smiled grimly. The flattery had done it; Bill had seen Monk expand when he had called him smart; it was characteristic of a man who wasn't.

The town was humming and people gave him plenty of elbow room. It was thought that, singlehanded, he had worsted two of the best gunmen in Calder and such a feat entitled him to respect.

THE *CLARION* office was lighted and Bill saw the five leaders of the Party inside. He went in. Molly turned her head and saw him and her face brightened.

"What's this Fred tells us? Did you really shoot two of Monk's men?"

"I'm afraid I did," admitted Bill with an apprehensive glance at Nancy. "One was a murderer and the other a horse thief."

"That's wonderful, Bill! That's two votes Malone won't get!"

Nancy's eyes were troubled. "It's two more murders; I'm afraid we won't enjoy a victory won at the cost of human lives."

Bill shook his head. "You women are funny. One praises me for shooting them and the other gives me—hail Columbia. But you're off in your count, Molly; Monk's lost fourteen votes in the last week."

"Fourteen!"

"That's right. The two dead ones, and the twelve that disappeared from Calder this week."

Sivart said, "Twelve? I thought it was only eight."

"More recent returns," grinned Bill. He had made a slip, for he wasn't supposed to know about the four that had disappeared the night before. But he was among friends.

"That certainly is good news," approved Fred. "Maybe Malone's men are beginning to see the handwriting on the wall; we're going to win that election tomorrow, Bill."

"Well, count noses right close, Fred, and if you're shy a few votes let me know. Excuse me, Nancy; I was just fooling."

"It isn't right, Bill," she told him. *"He that lives by the sword will perish by the sword."*

THAT Monday was a hectic day, both sides making their last minute efforts to convince voters. In Monk's case the word was intimidate rather than convince; he was sure of his votes, he strove to fix it so that the Cleanup Party wasn't sure of theirs. The free drink sign remained above the *Frontier* and the miners declared a holiday in order to take full advantage. They were drunk all over the place.

The Malone forces held a torchlight parade that night. They wore full regalia, including sixguns and rifles. It was very imposing. They were strung out in two long files and Bill suspected that many of them ducked into alleys and circled the block in order to pass in review a second time. At three o'clock in the morning the *Frontier* closed and drunken miners weaved their ways to the gulch or were helped there by roughs. Bill had never seen Malone's hardbitten criminals so gentle and tender-hearted; he suspected a purpose in their kindness but could not sense what it was.

He went to the polling place in Hollister's store bright and early on Tuesday morning. The election board had already assembled. For Malone there was a rough named Martin,

Joe Haynes of the *Gold Standard* and Blackie White, another saloon owner; for the Cleanup Party there were Leander Sexton, Reverend Rutherford and Molly. Molly handed Bill a printed sheet from a stack on the counter. He read it slowly.

The Cleanup Party's candidate for Mayor
Alfred Sivart
For Councilmen, Henry Hollister, Benjamin Shotten, Edward Wilson

So Sivart was the mystery candidate. Henry Hollister was the owner of the store, Shotten and Wilson were both miners.

A number of Malone's toughs hung around outside the store with the evident purpose of impressing voters. Tradesmen went in, cast their votes and came out again looking apprehensive or defiant according to their natures. There was a cluster of grim-faced women there, too, probably to make sure that the courage of their menfolk did not evaporate under the hot looks of the Malone crowd.

Bill prowled the town keeping eyes and ears open. He checked on Frank Cade at the *Double Eagle*, then found the cabin where the man lived, discovered that the back door was unlocked, and slipped inside and searched the place thoroughly. He found nothing to indicate that Cade was the power behind the throne occupied by Monk.

He missed Smoke Rafferty, and a bartender at the *Frontier* told him that the gunman was not in Malone's office. He didn't see Smoke all morning and the fellow's absence worried him; something was in the wind.

The town began to fill up after dinner. Cowboys came riding in, cast their votes, then went to the *Double Eagle*. Wes and his five would not be in until late in the afternoon. Malone's roughs drifted in and voted one or two at a time, stringing it out. Not one of the miners had come up from the gulch yet. Shortly after noon Monk Malone waddled into the store and voted. Smoke Rafferty was with him and Bill felt better.

Bill cast his own vote at around three in the afternoon, and when he came out of the booth Molly stopped him. "I'm getting worried about the miners," she told him. "It's getting late and we need their votes badly. What's keeping them?"

"Hangovers, I should guess. They'll be in before the polls close at sundown."

"They'd better be! Bill, why don't you ride down to the gulch and hurry them along."

He said he would and got his horse and rode down. The long toms were deserted and the whole settlement was as silent as the grave. He went into the first shack he came to and heard heavy snores before he had crossed the threshold. The miner was sprawled on his bunk, arms dangling, feet spread, snoring his life away.

Bill shook him and slapped him and got no response other than some thickly muttered words. He bent over and got a good whiff of the man's breath. It was laden with whiskey and something else. He sniffed at the tin-cup which had fallen from the man's hand to the floor. What was that alien smell? Laudanum?

He hurried to another shack and found the same condition. He also found it in the next, and the next, and the next. Miners were sprawled in bunks, in chairs, on floors. All of them slept the sleep of the dead; every one of them had been drugged.

And now Bill could make a good guess as to where Smoke Rafferty had been that morning. He had taken a liberal supply of doped whiskey to the gulch and had poured it into the gullets of miners still so drunk that they didn't know what they were drinking. And the loss of the miner vote meant the loss of the election to Molly and their followers.

BORDEN rode back to the store as quickly as horseflesh could carry him. "Looks like the Cleanup Party's sunk," he reported grimly to Molly. "Every miner in the gulch has been doped with doctored whiskey. They won't come out of it before night and then they won't even care who was elected."

The despair which came into her face made him wince. "But we've got to have their votes! We've got to get them up here!"

He said, "Where's Nancy?"

"At the Gospel tent, I suppose."

He turned to Hollister. "Grind up five pounds of coffee. I'll stop for it on my way back."

He rode up to the tent and told the story to Nancy. "We'll go down there and pour black coffee into them. We've got to get them on their feet and moving around. You have a horse and wagon; I'll hitch up and put the melodeon in it. We'll need it."

They stopped at the store long enough to get the coffee, then went on to the gulch, Nancy driving the wagon, Bill riding beside her. They built a fire in a stove and collected half a dozen coffeepots. Bill brewed the coffee and he brewed it strong enough to talk. Then they went to work.

Bill said to Nancy, "Get up on that wagon and play like hell!"

She went out and struck up, "Suzanna." Bill hauled a miner from his bunk and said, "Come on, partner, let's dance!" He pushed and pulled the doped man about the floor until at last the fellow began moving his own feet. It was quite a trick to get two of them together, but once he succeeded the two kept shuffling automatically.

He ran into another house, calling to Nancy as he did so to keep playing. Within another hour, feet were shuffling in a dozen shacks and Nancy was squeezing "Suzanna" out of the little organ for the sixtieth time.

After that it came easier. More coffee and profanity. Nancy started singing. Bill turned loose a violent tirade. "Listen to her! Singing and playing her heart out for a bunch of worthless bums! Are you going to let her down? Going to let Malone make suckers of you? Come on; get your feet tracking! Come up town and vote!"

They went. They followed the wagon in a stumbling, weaving procession, their very efforts sweating alcohol and drug from their bodies. Bill brought up in the rear like a drag rider behind a herd of cattle, urging, prodding, cursing. The sun was touching the horizon when they staggered down the street to the store. Wes and his cowboys came thundering to meet them, to give them protection if they needed it. They stumbled into the store—and voted.

Outside, a revolver barked to announce that the polls were closed. The election board counted the votes. Bill, standing in the doorway, heard Molly's excited cry of triumph, then saw her father climb to the top of a stepladder with a roll of canvas. He tacked a corner to the wall and started unrolling it. The word WIN? was revealed. The last letter of the winner's name came into view, then the next to the last.

A small cyclone hit Bill. Arms went about his neck and hugged him and a pair of lips smacked fervently against his cheek. Molly cried, "Bill, we did it! We did it! We won by six votes!"

Bill heard her as one in a dream. He was watching the banner unfold, and as he watched, the veil was lifted and he saw and understood and was dumb with astonishment and comprehension.

A small cheer went up from the Cleanup Party's supporters who could see the banner. The legend it bore was SIVART WINS!

∫ 14 ∫

Blood And Death

MOLLY was shaking him. "Bill! You're like a post! Don't you understand? We won!"

He blinked the cobweb from his brain and looked down at her. "Did we?"

"Of course! Can't you read? At any rate, I won; and you owe me a lifetime of service—dish washing, bed making, type cleaning— Bill, wake up!"

Bill looked over her shoulder and into the face of Fred Sivart. He said, "Congratulations, Sivart. Pretty close, wasn't it?"

Fred smiled with his lips. "Thanks. You helped a lot. Bill. You're a very resourceful man; myself and the members of the new council want you to continue as marshal if you will."

"Just until things settle down," He looked again at Molly. "You and Nancy better go somewhere where you'll be safe. There's no telling how Malone's crowd will take this."

Her chin went up. "I'm not afraid of them! We beat them with votes, we can beat them with guns."

"Don't be foolish," he said impatiently. "The miners will be no good to us if it comes to a fight. Fred, take them out to the Turner ranch, will you? It's the safest place I can think of."

Fred said, "Good idea. I'll do it."

Bill turned and hurried though the doorway. Malone's roughs had gone; he could see some of them running towards the Frontier with the news. Wes and his cowboys were there and Bill said, "I'm deputizing all of you. Come up to the *Double Eagle* and we'll gather all the hands we can; we're going to need them."

They rode up the street and Wes gave his report. Their prisoners had been delivered, they had snatched a few hours' sleep and had started back immediately.

"Sheriff give you any message for me?"

"Yes. Said what you expected hadn't come through yet, but should arrive at any minute—whatever it is."

"You'll find out later—I hope. Right now we got a job on our hands. Wes, I just tumbled to the whole setup and I'm still in a fog; I don't know how these roughs are going to react. It'll be in one of two ways: either they'll sit tight and won't make a move, or they'll start taking the town apart. If I got it figured out right, it'll be the latter."

Wes said, "Fine! That'll give us the chance we've been waitin' for ever since John Turner was shot—to shoot our way through the *Frontier*, drag Malone out of his office and hang him over the livery corral gate."

"Take it from me, that would be a mistake. Monk didn't originate the order to kill Turner or give the signal to Sam Sneed. All this time, Malone has been merely a front for somebody else."

"Who? Bill, you owe me that much! Who?"

Bill considered a moment. "I can't tell you yet, Wes; I think I know but I haven't proof. I've got to be certain before I turn you loose on him."

"Can I count on your lettin' us handle him when you have that proof?"

"You can. The law would doubtless execute him in any event, but you boys are entitled to the job and you'll have it. Right now do one thing for me; keep your eye on Frank Cade, every minute. And don't let him get away."

They dismounted before the *Double Eagle* and stood for a moment listening to the sounds which rolled across the street from the *Frontier*. They were ominous sounds—the babble of excited voices, the shuffling of excited feet, occasional angry oaths and shouts. There was no longer any doubt in Bill's mind; the roughs, realizing that they had lost their protection, were bent on wrecking the town before they scattered for the hills.

"We'd better hurry," said Bill. "And we'd better get our horses off the street."

They led the animals to the alley in back and left them there. They entered the *Double Eagle* by a rear door.

THE PLACE was crowded with celebrating cowboys and tradespeople and a few of the hardier miners. They were flushed with victory and were buying drinks as fast as the bartenders could fill their orders. Frank Cade sat at his layout, stony of face, idly shuffling a deck of cards. Bill thrust through the crowd, elbowed a man away from the bar and leaped to its surface. His violence and the grimness of his face caught their attention and they hushed.

He said, "Cut out the drinking. Malone's men are going on the warpath,

and we'll need every man, every gun, if we expect to stop them. The miners are out on their feet; they'll be of no use to us. You cowboys, get your horses off the street. Anybody who isn't packing a gun come with me to the jail and I'll distribute what weapons we have there. Fellows, I'm not fooling; within the next half hour Calder's going to live up to its reputation of being the 'Devil's Doorstep' and 'Hell's Back Yard.'"

It sobered them like a dash of icy water, and in the silence which followed they all heard the surge of sound from the *Frontier* and knew Bill was speaking truth. The cowboys left their drinks and went for their horses; Bill jumped from the bar and started for the door, a dozen men at his heels. They followed him across the street to the jail, and as they passed the *Lucky Tiger* another wave of sound pounded their ear drums. Bill unlocked the door and they went in and he handed weapons from the rack and then supplied them with ammunition from the desk.

And then there reached them a sudden outburst of increased sound—the wild yells of killers, the sudden thunder of sixguns and the sharper crack of rifles. In answer to it came yells of defiance and a scattered volley of gunshots.

Bill ran to the jail door. Up the street, outlaws were pouring from the doors of the *Frontier* and across the street in the direction of the *Double Eagle*. They fired as they ran, and answering shots blazed from the front of the *Double Eagle*, the orange stabs coming from the doorway and through front windows. Bill saw some of the outlaws stumble and fall before the mob split to right and left in search of cover.

He was about to call to his men to follow him when another mob burst from the *Lucky Tiger* next door. They wheeled to the right in the direction of the *Frontier*, but one of them, glancing over his shoulder, saw Bill and let out a yell of alarm. It was the last sound he made. Bill shot him dead, started thumbing the hammer of his Colt. Two more went down; then the mob had turned in its tracks and Bill leaped inside and slammed the heavy door as a gust of lead swept the place where he had been standing.

He yelled, "See that the back door is barred—quick!" and several men bolted through the corridor.

The jail was of adobe and as strong as a fort; there were two small front windows instead of a single big one. The panes to these went at once, but the windows were set high in the wall and nobody inside was hit.

Bill said, "You four with riot guns. get up to those windows and start throwing buckshot. Some of you others man the windows in the cells."

The door shook as heavy shoulders struck it, but it was solid and did not give. Lead continued to sweep through the windows and flatten on the adobe walls. In the back, other shoulders butted vainly against the rear door. Four of the men, crouching low, moved to the front windows. Still crouching below the sills, they shoved their sawed-off shotguns through the apertures and let fly. There were howls of rage and pain and the fire temporarily ceased. From the direction of the *Frontier* came the sounds of furious fighting.

BILL WENT back into the cell corridor. Men were standing on bunks at the small barred windows of the cells, sixguns ready. They were too high to see or do anything, but it would go hard with any outlaw who poked his head above the sills to try a shot. Two men stood with levelled rifles a few feet from the back door. Bill decided that this place could hold out indefinitely, but the *Frontier* was another matter.

Dusk had descended and was rapidly changing to darkness. He went back into the office and called two of the men with riot guns to him and led them through the corridor to the back door. He said, "I'm going out. I got to see how things are down the street. You boys cover me while I make for the stable. You with the rifle, take down the bar and unlock the door. In the rear cells, there! How does it look?"

A man peering through one of the small windows which overlooked the alley answered. "Five or six of 'em back here. One behind a barrel, two behind a wagon to the right of the stable, two more inside, and maybe one in the loft."

"Boys, you heard that. You men with the riot guns, put a barrel each into the stable door, then hold your fire. You fellows at the windows, watch the barrel and the wagon. One of you riflemen cover the loft. Now open up and let the riot guns do their stuff."

He crouched beside the door. It was yanked open suddenly and the two with the riot guns stepped up and fired their buckshot through the stable doorway. Pushing in front of them, crouching, Bill took off like a sprinter doing a hundred yard dash.

He made five of the ten yards between him and the doorway in a straight plunge, then started leaping zigzag fashion. A gun flashed from the blackness within the stable and he fired at the orange flame and heard a grunt of agony. Then he was in the doorway. The man at whom he had fired was to his right; the other would be to the left. He turned left and crashed solidly into a yielding body. He went down on top of the other and felt the burn of powder on his face as the man's gun exploded. He struck savagely with the barrel of his Colt, again and again. The last blow landed squarely and he felt and heard the squashy crack that told of a fractured skull.

He rolled clear and got to his feet, whirling to face the door. He saw one of his men raise his scatter gun and let fly at the upstairs, then wheeled as a man came scampering down the ladder from the loft. He was just an indistinct shadow and his back was turned to Bill; but Bill shot him without any compunction whatever.

He went on through the barn and came to the open ground in back of the stable. He stumbled along in the semi-darkness, managing to punch out the empty shells and reload as he ran. He filled the cylinder completely; no need now to keep an empty under the hammer.

He passed behind the *Lucky Tiger* and cut into the alley where the going was better. He continued along the alley towards the *Frontier* and suddenly smelled smoke. It was too dark to see where it originated, but it was somewhere ahead, he was sure.

He reached the *Frontier*, opened the back door and went inside; there were no lights and the place was as gloomy as a graveyard. Up towards the front some outlaws crouched below the windows, firing occasionally at the *Double Eagle* across the way. There was nobody in the back. He crossed to the office, turned the doorknob and went in.

He stepped to one side of the doorway and stood with his back to the wall and his Colt levelled, waist high, peering about in the blackness. He saw nothing, heard no sound. He moved over to Monk's desk, saw against the lighter darkness of the rear window that Monk was not there. He went around, sat down in the chair, struck a match with his left hand, holding the flame high so that the flash would not blind him. The office was empty.

Borden lighted the lamp and turned the wick low, then went through Monk's desk swiftly but efficiently. He found not a thing that would do him any good. He hadn't really expected to; Malone's desk would be the first thing to be examined after the Cleanup Party got in.

He blew out the light, went through the side door into the passageway beside the place, moved up to the front and, lying flat on the ground, looked across the street. Flashes came from the *Double Eagle* downstairs and up, but they were not as numerous or as continuous as he would have liked. Either the defenders had scattered and were holding their fire or they had suffered losses at the hands of Monk's roughs.

He went back into the alley and continued up it, and suddenly there was a bright glow against the sky and then flames leaped into the air. He ran. He stumbled over some rubbish,

swore, got up and rounded into the street. It was dark now and forms were but vague shadows that he could not recognize.

IT WAS Hollister's store which was afire, and there was a mob of crazy dancing figures before it. More figures were running in and out of the store, and those who came out were loaded down with merchandise. The fire was in the back of the building.

As Bill approached he saw a torch break into flame. The man who held it ran up the steps and into the store, and by its light Bill recognized him. Forgetting personal danger, he thrust his way through the shouting outlaws. In their excitement they seemed not to recognize him.

He went up the steps at a run and nearly stumbled over a sprawled body at their top. He stooped and rolled the man over. He was Hank Hollister and he had been shot through the head. Bill leaped over the body and went into the store.

Bolts of cloth had been unrolled and piled in the middle of the floor and the reek of kerosene was in the air. The man ahead of him hurled the burning torch into its midst and it went up with a great *woosh!*

Smoke Rafferty wheeled to run for the door and in the blaze recognized Bill. He froze in midstride, a black silhouette against the flames. He was caught flatfooted, for Bill's gun was levelled at him and his own Colt was still in its holster.

His hands went into the air. "Don't shoot! I give up!"

Bill said, "No you don't; shoot, you stinking little reptile!"

He slid his gun into its holster and raised his hands to the same level as Rafferty's.

He couldn't see the expression on the man's face, but he knew what it was. It reflected despair turned suddenly into triumph, resignation into gloating. The fool marshal was going to play his game and Rafferty was sure he could not lose; Smoke's hands swept down with the speed of a lightning bolt.

Bill hands moved every bit as fast. Years of training sent the right one unerringly to the walnut butt of the Colt, then back and down in a quick jerk that swiveled the holster upward. The Colt roared through the open bottom of the holster and Smoke's bullet ploughed into the floor at Bill's feet.

Smoke staggered backwards, his arms outflung as though he were trying to recover his balance; but the slug had gone through his brain and he was already dead. He fell into the blazing pile and Bill walked forward as close as he could. He said, "Burn, you killer! I couldn't dream up a better end for you if I tried."

Slugs started whining through the front door and Bill knew his way to safety was closed as far as the front was concerned. The back was blazing fiercely. He ran to a side window, smashed out sash and pane with his Colt, got through it and dropped to the ground. He was in just as bad a position as he had been inside the store, for the heat in the rear of the narrow passage was too intense to let him through and outlaws were in the front of the store.

He moved forward grimly; he'd have to shoot his way through.

And then he heard the pound of hoofs and the sudden roar of guns, and the forms of running outlaws began to appear as they sped by the passageway. They looked back over their shoulders and some of them paused to wheel and fire. Some of them went down.

Bill ran to the corner, adding his fire to that of the horsemen. He was grinning now, and as they swept up he ran out, waving his hands to attract their attention.

"Where the hell you been?" he roared at them. "You were supposed to be here not later than sundown."

"That you, Cap?" called one of the Rangers. "Looks like you're havin' some fun for yourself."

The whole company pulled up. Bill said drily, "Yeah. Too bad you showed up so soon; I was just about to polish the rest of 'em off."

"Took the wrong road and went twenty miles out of the way. This is the dangdest country I ever seen; take an Injun guide to get you through. But we knew you were on the job so we didn't worry none."

"Don't try to cover up with flattery, you grinning ape. Give me one of your stirrups and I'll climb up behind you. Straight down the street and shoot everything that doesn't throw down his shooting iron and push the hands in the air. Ride on, brave one; I'm right behind you."

"Yeah," said the other. "That's the trouble!"

∫ 15 ∫

Gateway To Heaven

THE Turner ranch house was the scene of uneasy quiet. The only occupants who were not uneasy were the children, and they were in bed.

Inside the house, Mrs. Turner moved about silently, srtaightening furniture, opening and closing closets, peering often through the open door towards the rosy sky which told of flames in Calder. In a chair by the table, Reverend Rutherford read his Bible, but it was difficult to concentrate and he found his eyes drawn often to the ruddy glow.

Out on the gallery Molly Sexton and Nancy Rutherford sat in chairs, Nancy stiff and tense, Molly restless and fearful. Leander Sexton rocked jerkily. Fred Sivart paced up and down, tense, nervous, his glance rarely leaving the reflection in the sky.

"It's awful, awful!" said Nancy in a stricken voice. "And we thought all the fighting, all the trouble was over. Oh, why must men do such wicked things!"

"So that good men like Bill must

undo them," said Molly sharply. "And get killed doing it." Her voice had the note of hysteria in it.

Nancy said, "You love him, don't you, Molly?"

"Of course. Don't you?"

"I like him very much. In some ways he reminds me— There was another Bill, Molly. He was big and curly-headed and laughing. But they —they shot him. There'll never be another one for me."

"Nancy, how horrible! I'm so sorry." Molly impulsively put her arms about the little blonde girl.

Fred Sivart had turned. Now he came over to stand looking down at Molly. When he spoke his voice was harsh. "What's that you said about Bill? That you loved him?"

"Yes. I think I always have. He's the darndest man; he torments me and makes me mad, and he's always so darned right; but I love him, and what's more I told him so."

"You told him?"

"Sure. You saw me kiss him there at the store, didn't you?"

"Yes. But I doubt if he knew it. Or was it the kiss that brought that dazed look to his face?"

"I hope so; if it wasn't I'll keep on trying until it does."

"If you're so set on getting your man, why don't you join the Rangers?" sneered Sivart.

Nancy said matter of factly, "I believe Bill's a Ranger."

That jolted them. Molly gasped and her father said, "What?"

Fred Sivart snapped, "What makes you think that?"

"He's so efficient, so closemouthed, so calm, so sure. And what brought him to Calder in the first place? He's no idle drifter, much less a fugitive from the law."

Sexton said, "But I wrote to the Rangers appealing for help; and your father wrote directly to the Governor. All we got in reply was the vague promise of help sometime in the dim future."

Molly's eyes were bright. "What did you expect, Dad? A definite promise that a company of Rangers would arrive at ten A.M. on October 25th? You'd print it in the *Clarion* and the whole flock would be tipped off."

"Somebody coming!" said Sivart in a sharp voice. He was leaning out over the edge of the gallery, his head cocked like that of a setter.

"Maybe it's Malone's roughs!" cried Sexton. "We'd better go inside."

A distant shout came ringing over the range. "*Yip! Yip! Yip-eee!*"

"That's Wes," announced Mrs. Turner from the doorway. "He always lets out that yell when he sights the house."

"We'll learn the worst now," said Sexton in a tight voice.

Rutherford had followed Mrs. Turner to the door. "That was not a cry of defeat," he said, his voice ringing. "That was a shout of triumph! I know it; I feel it! My friends, the Lord is with us!"

THEY RODE up with a great clatter, and as they dismounted Molly cried, "Bill!" and flung herself at him. And this time he wasn't too dazed to realize that he held one hundred and ten pounds of desirability in his arms and her fervent kiss did not go unanswered.

There was another man with Wes and his cowboys. He was blackhaired and blackcoated and once he had been suave. Right now he bestrode a horse with his hands bound to the saddle horn and he looked rather the worse for wear. One of the men untied him and dragged him from the horse and he was herded into the house with the rest of them.

Bill was hatless, his face was dirty and powder streaked, and a thin trickle of blood had dried on one cheek; but his eyes sparkled and there was an air of supreme satisfaction about him.

Wes said, "Folks, meet up with Captain Bill Borden of the Rangers. He sure had us fooled to a fare-you-well. But Rangers don't talk until the job is done. The Governor sent him in answer to Reverend Rutherford's letter to sort of look the ground over and get things lined up so that the boys could come in and gather 'em into the fold without wastin' any time. And, boy, did they gather 'em!"

He told his openmouthed listeners of the battle in Calder and its dramatic climax. The store was gone; so was Hank Hollister and one of the miners who had been elected councilman. Several of the cowboys had been killed, and a number of them wounded. More than a dozen outlaws had been killed, twice that many wounded, and the jail and livery corral held the rest, guarded by the Rangers.

"What about Malone?" asked Sexton.

Bill answered. "We gathered him in, too; found him hiding under a bed. Might have missed him, but he's so fat that the bed bulged. But Malone wasn't the main one; he was only a front. Just before this protection racket started, a suave stranger moved into Calder; he was an outlaw named Al Travis, wanted for murder a couple times over. He started the protection racket, but he didn't want to attract attention to himself so he used Monk and the *Frontier* and paid Malone a percentage."

They all looked at Frank Cade. Sexton said, "So it was him all the while; he worked for Fred and learned things—secrets of the Clean-up Party. He was a councilman, and used his position to keep in touch with Monk Malone, who was mayor. Yes, it's all very plain now."

"I don't think it is," said Bill quietly. "Cade was the messenger, all right, but he isn't Al Travis. He fits the description somewhat, but he hasn't a six-inch knife scar on his chest. Grab him, fellows!"

For Fred Sivart had started to edge away, his glinting eyes on Bill and and his hand on the butt of his Colt. He backed right into the hands of two cowboys, who promptly grabbed him and held him while Wes stepped forward and took his gun.

Sivart said, "Let me go! The man's crazy!"

"Not as crazy as you wish I was," Bill told him grimly. He took a wanted notice from his pocket, unfolded it and read:

Age, 26. That fits. Height, 5 feet 11 inches. That fits. Weight, 175. Just right. Color of hair, blond. A shampoo'll fix that up. Eyes, blue. Check. Six-inch knife scar on chest." Bill reached out and with one jerk tore open the man's ruffled shirt.

Sivart—or Travis—struggled then. He struggled fiercely, silently; but the rest of the cowboys jumped him and he was subdued and held rigid while Bill tore open the silk undershirt. On his chest was a livid knife-scar, just about six inches long.

BILL WENT on. "From the very first I realized that Monk was fronting for somebody. He was too slow-witted to handle a scheme of such proportions. I finally settled on Cade, for the reasons given by Mr. Sexton. It wasn't until the canvas was unrolled after the voting that I tumbled to the truth. You unrolled it from right to left, Mr. Sexton, tacking it in place as it opened. The first word we saw was WINS! Then came Sivart's name, letter by letter, but reversed. First the T, then the R, then the rest of it. And right before my eyes was unrolled the name that had caught my attention when first I looked at the reward notice. My first glance must have caught that name backwards, too; but I didn't get it then. To you folks that banner read SIVART WINS! To me the name was TRAVIS... All right, boys. Hate to wish the trip on you, but you'd better take him to Calder and turn him over to the Rangers, I'll bring Cade in later; he'll have lots to tell."

They hustled Travis from the room and put him on the horse Cade had ridden. They roped him securely and took the added precaution of slipping the noose of a lariat about his neck.

When they were at a safe distance from the house, Wes said, "Well, I reckon we'll have to pick up a tree with nice strong limbs. We can't use the livery corral gate; the Rangers might not like it."

Travis said, "You're—not—?" His voice was a croak.

"We sure are," said Wes grimly. "You dirty rat! You planned John's death; it was you that waved the signal to Sam Sneed. Bill promised he'd let us take care of you, but he had to throw a bluff because he's a lawman. And we'll help him keep up his bluff. After you're good and dead we aim to fill you full of lead and report, very sadly, that you got shot tryin' to escape. I never thought I'd enjoy lynchin' a man; but hangin' fellers like Sam Sneed and you gives me the greatest kind of pleasure."

Back in the house, Bill was finishing the explanation. "Towards the end Travis began to doubt that Malone would carry the election, so he fixed things so that he'd be certain to remain in control of the town. He pushed himself forward in the Cleanup Party and got himself made candidate. Even in winning you'd lose, for in a short while he'd start the protection racket all over; and with your own mayor a crook you'd never be able to stage a comeback.

"He didn't bother about the councilmen. When one dies while in office, the mayor appoints a successor to serve his time out. All he had to do was bump two of 'em off, put his own men in, and he'd have a majority. Tonight Holister and another of your councilmen were killed, right off the bat.

"I didn't know at first how the roughs would take it. If he took 'em into his confidence, they'd have just sat tight and grinned. But he didn't dare take the chance of telling them, and he'd already collected for their protection. It didn't matter how many of them were killed off; there'd be plenty of fresh ones to take their places."

Nancy came up to him and extended her hand. She smiled up at him as he gingerly held it. "God bless you, Bill," she said. "I suppose your methods were justified, for even the Lord used force at times."

"Thanks, Nancy. You helped a lot yourself. If you had just kept on marching and singing you could have led those fool miners plumb to the gateway of Heaven." He released her hand and turned to Molly. "Let's go out on the gallery, Reporter, and cook up a story for the *Clarion*. You'll be working for me now; I own it."

THEY HAD started for the gallery, but Molly halted. "You do not! We won the election!"

"You put a murderer in as mayor; I figure that Malone won any way you look at it."

They went out on the dark gallery. They were alone. She said, "Bill you always twist things around to suit you. You won't admit when you're licked."

He laughed happily. "Oh, yes, I will. I'm licked right now, lady. I'm going to give you that lifetime of service. Of course, I'll have to resign from the Rangers, but a Borden never welches on his bets."

She said rapturously, "Bill! Bill!" and flung her arms about him.

After a while he pushed her from him. "Hey! How about that ring? You're still wearing it!"

"The engagement ring?" she said innocently. "Why shouldn't I wear it? Every once in a while I get sentimental and put it on. I love it; it was my mother's, you see."

He drew her to him again. "I see where we're going to have lot of fun tormenting each other through life."

He slipped his arm about her and pulled her to the edge of the gallery. Off towards Calder the sky still showed a faint tinge of red.

He said, "The fire at the 'Devil's Doorstep' is dying down and we won't be hearing that name any more. It's all wrong, anyhow; it never was that. Calder's the gateway to Heaven, because I met you there."

THE END

A true story of the Old West.

Pop-Zimco Printer

by REX WHITECHURCH

(Author of "Daughters of the Western Dance Halls")

*He never stayed very long at any job but Pop Zimco was
remembered wherever he went.*

POP ZIMCO was a hobo printer who traveled from cowtown to mining camp and never very long in one place. He was a good printer and his services were always in demand wherever there was a newspaper. Most of the more important western towns had publications, small

ones true, but they appeared regularly about once a week. The subscription price was usually five dollars a year— sometimes more, sometimes a little less. Pop could throw a stick of type together faster than any man in the business, according to some of the old time editors for whom he worked.

He'd save up his money and always stage a good drunk before he left town for the next stop. The longest he ever worked at one place, so say the records, was four weeks and this at Dodge City in 1874.

Pop was a small man, bald and he always wore a heavy gun strapped to a cartridge belt around his waist. He was amazingly fast on the draw, but he never flourished the gun unless it was necessary. One day in Dodge a band of soldiers who had been drinking caught the old man crossing the street in the rain and mud, and one tripped him. Pop rolled over and over and came up shooting. His gun appeared in his fist before anyone saw the movement of his hand. He fired five shots and the soldiers ran, but not before Pop had got the right forefinger of a soldier's hand. They never bothered him again in Dodge.

Pop's excuse for carrying the gun was his fear of being made to drink something he didn't want to drink or to dance when he didn't want to dance. But Link Caldwell of Hayes Kansas, found out the real reason. Pop was looking for a man, a man who had swindled him out of his newspaper at Pattonsburg, Mo. He'd once been in the money, but he'd fallen for a swindle as old as the hills.

The man had come along with a map on which was a spot he called Treasure Trove. The map told how to reach the buried gold, thirty thousand that road agents had buried in 1860. He told Pop he knew the money was there, and if it wasn't, Pop could have his shop back. But soon as Pop left town the man sold the shop and skipped.

Sounded simple, but it worked. Pop wasn't a fool, but he'd been caught off guard; he went out west and found the spot on the map and he dug for the money. He did find a saddle bag, rotted and buried deep in the exact place described on the map. But somebody had beaten him to the money. He had given the swindler power of attorney, to run his business in his absence, and if he found the gold he'd promised to remain lost to Pattonsburg and never demand his shop back.

That made a bum out of Pop Zimco, but he kept traveling from town to town, setting type and barmed with the heavy gun. He'd practiced for hours on drawing the pistol from the holster which he'd wear thonged down to his thigh. A little man with a big gun, they said.

Pop liked to write obituaries. He would compose them as he went along, carrying everthing in his head and setting the type to speak the eloquence in his mind. They say he wrote some four hundred obituaries, for friends and others who paid him his services because they wanted something nice said about their late lamented.

One of Pop's favorite epitaphs which stood on a Boothill Gravestone said,

Here's to Andy Bate
He drew but he was too late.

Pop never found his man. But he worked on thirty some odd newspapers in Denver and Topeka and throughout Utah and Wyoming and Colorado. Dodge City was always glad to see old Pop Zimco, and he returned there four times before he died.

Pop met his death in a cyclone near Hayes, Kansas. He was driving a team of mules to a small covered wagon when the storm struck. This was Pop's portable print shot. He'd saved his money for months and had been sober a long time, they say, when he was caught in the furious storm and crushed to death under the wreckage of his wagon. Pop made a living printing handbills and reward posters for lawmen. His portable print shot was one of the first traveling affairs of its kind known to the west. He got out a little newspaper which he'd circulate in shops and saloons carrying advertising for the merchants. But there seldom were more than two issues put out in the same town. All in all, Pop Zimco was doing quite well when he got in the way of that twister.

(Continued On Page 97)

Dudley and the sheriff had been separated.

Pretty Boy

by VAL GENDRON

(Author of "An Ace Up His Sleeve")

Will Dudley's resemblance to the notorious Pretty Boy Chauncey was dangerous to outlaws as well as to himself!

WILL DUDLEY'S gay, debonair manner had not deserted him even though he *was* tired and dirty. He hadn t slept in a bed, or undressed for two days; he was hungry—no one had bothered to tell him in Topeka that he had better carry provisions on the newly constructed Sante Fe to Wichita. He fingered the money-belt at his waist; his Uncle Ephriam's eighty thousand dollars was still safe.

The creeping train jerked to a stop along side an abondoned construction camp. The conductor poked his head in the coach. "All out!" he bawled.

"Is this Wichita?" Will asked in amazement.

"Naw," his seat-partner replied disdainfully. "But this is as far as this train goes."

With resignation Will hefted his carpet bag. "What do we do now?"

His travelling companion chewed reflectively on his wad of tobacco and regarded Will as if he were some outlandish visitor f r o m another planet.

"We wait for another train," The man explained patiently. He was eager to get away from Will as rapidly as possible.

This trip West was supposed to be a punishment devised by Uncle Ephriam because, after a night of dancing, Will had been too sleepy-eyed to distinguish a three from an eight —a fatal error in Uncle Ephriam's Boston bank. Will grinned; aside from the heat and the flies, and the physical discomfort which he didn't mind, the trip had turned out to be no punishment at all; he was fascinated by the country, and was looking forward to spending his Uncle Ephriam's eighty thousand dollars buying Texas cattle with enthusiasm.

He climbed down from the train, stepped aside to let a work-worn woman with half a dozen children clinging to her skirts pass. Instantly he found himself sprawling face down in the mud.

Behind him he heard raucous laughter. He turned slowly, wiping the muck from his face. "Hi, greenhorn!"

The man who stood over him was roughly dressed and unshaved. His eyes were narrow, mocking slits in his face. Will rose to his feet "Was that quite necessary?" he asked in clipped Boston accents.

His question brought another roar of laughter from the idlers. "Get your pretty clothes all mussed up?" the ringleader shouted.

Will looked down at his trousers. They had once been a soft, dove grey; they represented exactly what the well dressed young man about Boston was wearing these days. His anger suddenly melted; these were not exactly the clothes for Kansas, and a joke was a joke. Will didn't particularly mind if it was on him. "Maybe," he remarked drily, "they're more appropriate this way."

The others laughed with him, but the eyes of the ringleader were still cold and mean. He put his hand against Will's chest and shoved. "We don't like strangers around here!"

This time Will did not go sprawling. He dropped his carpet bag and regained his balance. "Now look here!" he exclaimed sharply.

An instant later he found himself looking down the barrels of a couple of .44's that had magically appeared in the bully's hands.

Cold fury seethed inside Will. He hated and despised a bully. It was the first time in his life he had ever met brute force in the hands of a ruthless opponent. He shrugged his shoulder; "Your hand," he said coldly.

The big man laughed. "It's always my hand, Bud." Then he walked off.

THE OTHER men moved away now the sport was over, and Will regarded him ruefully. He wondered what the outcome would have been if the big man had known he carried eighty thousand dollars strapped to his waist. After due reflection he decided it was a good thing his cattle-buying mission wasn't known; but someday, he figured, he'd meet the fellow on more equal terms.

He tightened his belt against the gnawing pangs of hunger. Sometime another train would come along and Will hoped it would get to the deserted construction camp before he died of starvation. In the meantime he could wash away the worst of the dirt and shave off his two days' beard.

He was sitting on the ground, a little travelling mirror gripped between his knees, and the long razor gliding smoothly over his chin, when he heard the sharp gasp of surprise and fright behind him.

Will started, nicked himself, and saw a pair of dazzlingly blue eyes in an astonishingly pretty face reflected in the mirror's surface.

He jumped to his feet in time to see the girl running back toward the center of camp as fast as her well shaped legs showing beneath her full skirt would carry her.

The West was an amazing place for a young Bostonian. First bullies shoved you in the mud, and when you objected confronted you with a brace of .44's. But the most disconcerting thing about the West was that the only pretty girl he had seen so far, ran from him in terror. Will never had gotten that reaction from Boston's young ladies.

If the other train didn't arrive for an hour or so he'd have plenty of time to meet the young charmer when half his face wasn't covered with lather. He started to finish shaving.

He was wiping the last of the lather from his ear when he heard a voice behind him. "All right, Chauncey; this is the end of the trail. I've got you covered, and I want to see your hands in the air."

Will was unpleasantly aware that this astonishing statement was addressed to him. The voice was authorative, the sort of voice one never argued with. Will raised his hands without question.

"Okay, turn around."

Will turned. He found himself face to face with a rangy, middle-aged man who wore a sheriff's star pinned to his worn vest. Beside him was the girl Will had caught a fleeting glimpse of in his mirror.

"That's him, Pa. Isn't it?"

"Yep, it's him," the sheriff replied. He regarded Will soberly. "Saw you on the train and didn't recognize you; you'd have been safe enough, if you hadn't bothered to shave."

"I think there's some mistake," Will said calmly. He wasn't afraid of a sheriff with a gun; this man looked reasonable and sane. Besides, back in Boston the police represented law and order and were a respectable enough segment of the human race. "I'm Will Dudley of Boston, Massachusetts; my papers are in my carpet bag."

The sheriff listened to Will's clipped accent. "That's a pretty good line," he grinned, "but I'm not buying it; get his gun, Sally."

Sally patted his pockets expertly, found the little pearl-handled pistol his Uncle Ephriam had given him. Next to the heavy .44 the sheriff held in his hand it looked like a child's toy.

"So," the Sheriff smiled. "Even for a get-away you couldn't leave your toys behind. Still carrying the little pearl one without any notches?"

Will sighed. "Before you go any further with this game that I don't understand, won't you look at my papers?"

"Don't you know when the game's up?" the Sheriff countered.

"The laughter," Will replied, "will be on my side when you bring in the wrong man." He said it so confidently that the Sheriff was impressed.

"What papers?"

"The letters of identification my uncle gave me to men in Wichita to enable me to buy eighty thousand dollars worth of Texas cattle coming up the trail."

"Eighty thousand dollars was what Pretty Boy Chauncey got from the Allandale Bank just two weeks ago," the sheriff said flatly.

"I can't help it," Will retorted. "I can't help it if he's six foot two, weighs a hundred and eighty, has a Boston tailor and has the same coloring and features I have; I'm not Pretty Boy Chauncey and I never heard of him before."

THE SHERIFF nodded philosophically. "You hit it on the head, straight down the line. You fit his description to the Tee. And if you ain't Pretty Boy, who in the hell are you?"

"I'm William C. Dudley from Boston. I'm here on business for my Uncle Ephriam; he sent me to buy Texas cattle, just like I told you."

Keeping his gun leveled on Will, the Sheriff turned to his daughter. "I *did* hear some Eastern banking fellow was expected along this way to buy up that herd that's moving north. Maybe you better look at those papers this gent keeps talking about."

"In my carpet bag," Will directed.

Sally ruffled through his belongings, tossing shirts and linen out recklessly. "Hey, be careful of my clothes," he cried.

"The outstanding thing about Pretty Boy Chauncey," Sheriff O'Neill said slowly, "is he's so damn particular about his clothes. Quite the ladies' man, too, so they say."

Will grinned a little wanly. "According to my Uncle Ephriam, it's me you're describing; he doesn't think much of my activities in that direction."

"He's probably right," Sheriff O'Neill laughed. "I didn't use to think so, but now that I've got a pretty daughter, I don't much favor the boys who are handy with the girls. It's all in the point of view. Find those papers yet, Sally?"

Will Dudley liked Sheriff O'Neill and liked hs daughter. He had liked O'Neill from the minute he looked into the lawman's frank, honest eyes. He was not a mean, little figure like Uncle Ephriam to quibble over whether a figure was a three or an eight; after this stupid mistake was straightened out, Will rather thought he and Sheriff O'Neill would get on well together.

Sally handed the bundle of letters to her father and he turned the gun over to her while he examined them. Will had an idea the weapon would be nowhere so dangerous in the hands of so charming an antagonist and he made the mistake of relaxing a little.

"Reach!" her voice was a feminine imitation of her father's. "I'm as good a shot as Pa, and I've no qualms about shooting no-good, lawless trash!"

Will reached high.

SHERIFF O'Neill put down the papers at last. "I'll tell you what, son. They look genuine, but you're the spit and image of Pretty Boy. There's one way to settle it, if you've a mind to; Pretty Boy has a scar from a knife wound on his left side he got down South of the border 'fore he came up this way Suppose you take your shirt off and let's see your side."

Will glanced at Sally. "Right here?"

"'Tain't the Boston Common, son. Sally won't mind your taking your shirt off."

Will turned to Sally. "Can I take my hands down to take off my shirt?"

Sheriff O'Neill guffawed loudly. "Sort of hope you ain't Pretty Boy; hate to have to take you in."

With considerable embarrassment Will took off his shirt and let them examine his left side.

"Satisfied?" he asked curtly.

In reply Sheriff O'Neill took a worn wallet from his pocket and showed him a much creased paper. It might have been his own picture there. Across the bottom ran the legend: *$20,000 Reward. Dead or Alive.*

"I'm the Sheriff of Wichita, and this picture ought to tell you how the mistake happened."

To Will's amazement Sally just sat down on a large rock and began to cry.

"Don't mind her," the Sheriff said. "She was kinda counting on that reward. Not so much for the money, but the prestige. You see I'm getting along in years, and back in Wichita there's some talk about how a younger man might be better for the job. Of course," he admitted, "if you'd turned out to be the man we took you for, all that talk'd die down."

"I'm almost sorry I'm not," Will said good-naturedly.

"You oughta be glad," Sheriff O'Neill replied. "There's a necktie party waiting him." He made a simple graphic gesture, and Will was very glad he wasn't Pretty Boy.

"Give him back that silly gun," the Sheriff told his daughter. "Maybe Sally can do the apologies better than I can, and make it up to you. And if I was you, I'd keep my lip buttoned about that eighty thousand dollars. This is still a raw country; money like that attracts trouble."

"You can make it up right now," Will interrupted. "I came from Topeka without anything to eat, and I'd be very grateful if you could spare me something."

"A real greenhorn!" the Sheriff laughed and Sally smiled prettily. Will thought her smile a good deal superior to the Boston variety.

"There'll be a train about sundown," Sally said, "and beside fixing you with supper, maybe you'll give us the pleasure of your company the rest of the way. I'd like to hear about Boston. My mother came from Vermont."

When she wasn't being business-like behind a gun, Sally had a most agreeable voice.

* * *

MAYBE IT was his appetite, or maybe it was Sally's cooking, Will couldn't decide, but he thought he'd never eaten a better meal.

The hours until the train came passed as quickly as the previous two days had passed slowly. Will forgot the heat and the flies and the discomfort. He was very well pleased with the world, and the O'Neill's, father and daughter, and he was equally well pleased with himself. He smiled to think how infuriated his Uncle Ephriam would be if he knew the trip he had devised as a punishment had turned out so well; the only thing he hadn't liked in this big new country was the rough who'd shoved him in the mud.

A train chugged in with considerable self-importance just at sundown. "Service is awful," Sheriff O'Neill said apologetically. "Trains run any old time, and even when they run we have trouble with bandits and train robbers. It's still a raw country. But to us old-timers who came out in ox-carts and wagons, this seems like the very height of progress.

Once aboard Will pulled his hat down far over his eyes, and followed the example of the others trying to get some sleep. He fell asleep almost at once.

His dreams were confused. There were pictures of his Uncle Ephriam's counting house, where three's and eight's mocked him. There were many pretty girls running away from him and when they turned and looked back over their shoulders they all had Sally O'Neill's features. There was the hurrying series of pictures of the country he was travelling through. It was a good country. A man's country where no silly figures danced derisively before his eyes. It was a fine country full of Sally O'Neill's.

He woke with a start to a series of shots exploding in his ears. He opened his eyes in time to see the bully who had shoved him in the mud shooting out the lights over the doors. "This is it, folks," his rough voice rang out. "Raise your hands high!"

"That's Luke Billings," Sheriff O'Neill whispered in his ear. "He's the boss of the Billings gang and a mighty tough customer. Specializes in this sort of thing." He laughed a little ruefully.

"This is just about going to finish me off with the good folks of Wichita. Imagine robbing a train with the Sheriff fast asleep aboard."

Sally turned to him. "Don't you worry, Pa; someday you'll show them."

Never in all Will Dudley's quiet, regulated life in Boston had he been faced with a situation like this. If anyone had asked him what he would do in a train robbery, he would probably have replied, "Give in peacefully."

But the Western air, or Sally's pretty face, had had a remarkable effect on him. He edged sideways behind Sheriff O'Neill so that his right hand was hidden. Very slowly he lowered his hand to his pocket, closed it over the little pearl-handled pistol. There was a long chance, that would pay the bully off for what he had done to him and save Sally's father at the same time.

The pistol fitted comfortably in Will's big fist. His voice, with the clipped Boston accent carried easily through the silent car. "Lay off, Billings," he said clearly. "This is my push."

THE OUTLAW turned, recognition dawning slowly in his narrow eyes. "Where'd you come from?" he demanded.

"I've been aboard all along," Will answered coldly. "You shoved me in the mud yesterday, remember?"

"M' Gosh!" Luke Billings sounded almost awed.

"I don't like being pushed around." Will swallowed with difficulty. "Care to shoot it out now?"

The big man shook his head slowly. "Look, Pretty Boy," his eyes shifted constantly from one end of the train to the other. "You're playing a lone hand. I got ten men on this job. One of 'em will be coming through that door behind you in a minute, then you'll be between two fires."

"Then," Will interrupted, "I might just as well plug you now."

"Maybe we could make a deal," Luke suggested.

This was exactly what Will had been hoping for. "What kind of a deal?"

"I'll split you in with us. We'll divide the take evenly between all of us."

"How much do you figure to take from this train?" Will asked.

"We ought to get a couple of thousand dollars," Luke frowned.

"Divided among eleven men!" Will laughed. "You take big risks for small profits. I got a better idea."

"Yeah?" There was skepticism in the outlaw's tone.

Will leaned easily against the side of the car. His plan was going to work; he was perfectly confident of it. It was a risky thing to try, but the danger only stirred his blood. "You know, there never was a jail built tight enough to hold me. I understand there's a twenty thousand dollar reward out for me."

"Dead or alive," Luke Billings put in.

Will shook his head. "Only alive, my friend; ask the Sheriff here."

Sheriff O'Neill's face was a puzzle and Sally's eyes were deep, frightened pools in her white face. But despite his bewilderment the Sheriff nodded confirmation of Will's claim.

"I suppose you've got horses around here?" Will went on.

Luke Billings nodded.

"Okay. Here's what we do. Have your men return whatever they took from the passengers, so you have no criminal charges against you. Then take the Sheriff along with you and ride into Wichita where he'll pay you the reward and no questions asked. My own safety," he winked significantly at Luke, "you can leave entirely up to me.

The outlaw wetted his lips, greed fighting with craft in his transparent mind as he tried to figure out whether it was a trap.

"It's twenty thousand sure," Will put in, "against the couple of thousand you can get from this train."

Luke scratched his chin. "There was a rumor some Eastern guy was coming out carrying heavy cash to buy up that herd moving north out of Texas. We was hoping he was on this train."

"Oh," Will smiled but his eyes remained hard and cold. "Holding out on me, with that silly story about only taking a couple of thousand from this train, heh?"

"Not exactly," Luke admitted grudgingly. "We ain't found him yet."

IT OCCURRED to Will that posing as an outlaw might save his Uncle Ephriam's eighty thousand

dollars, though that had not been his intention at all. The money had been a detail that escaped his attention while he was concentrating on a way to help Sheriff O'Neill and put Luke Billings where he belonged, behind bars. There was a grim humor to the situation that appealed to Will.

"If you find him," Will said quietly, "let me know. I'll be waiting."

Just then one of the Billings Gang appeared through the other door of the car. "Not in any of the other cars. Find him here?" he asked.

"No," Luke grinned. "But I found Pretty Boy Chauncey and he'll prove just as good."

"Pretty Boy!" the other moved forward.

Will did not change the position of his gun, or take his eyes from Luke Billings. "Any smart moves," he warned, "and you get it first."

Luke Billings shifted uneasily. Once again he scratched his rough chin. "Always heard you were a pretty tough customer."

"Tough enough," Will replied, "to play this game alone. You need ten men to help you, so I'm just nine times tougher than you are and don't forget it."

"Okay, okay." Luke Billings' voice was no more than a grumble.

Sheriff O'Neill spoke up quickly. "Don't forget to return what you took from these people so there are no charges against you," he warned.

Luke gave the orders gruffly, while, under his breath, Sheriff O'Neill whispered to Will, "Are you crazy?"

"Like a fox," Will grinned. "Once back in Wichita you can clamp this crew in your jailhouse. I'll arrive safe and sound with Uncle Ephriam's cash; it's really very simple."

"Yeah," Sheriff O'Neill sneered. "If they don't catch on, and you and I both get to Wichita alive."

"I fooled them, didn't I?" Will asked.

He wasn't worried. It was the first time in his life that Will Dudley had acted according to his instincts and he liked the way he felt. He decided in that instant that Boston was no place for him. He belonged here in the West where a man could take his fate in his own hands and stand on his own two feet. He rather imagined there was a place for him in Wichita.

"They'll kill us both if they ever find out," Sheriff O'Neill shrugged.

Sally's eyes blazed in her white face. "I almost think he fooled us, Pa. I think maybe he's Pretty Boy after all."

Her father regarded her sobeily. "What about the scar?" he asked.

"That's the sort of trick Pretty Boy would pull," she said slowly. "That description of him came from somebody who was supposed to be a pal of his turned informer. Maybe Pretty Boy had him circulate that story, so if he was ever caught he could get out of it. Just like this fellow did."

Sheriff O'Neill studied Will thoughtfully. "What about it, son?"

Before Will could say anything, Luke Billings interrupted sharply. "What are you and the Sheriff so friendly about?"

"Just asking what sort of meals he serves in his establishment," Will laughed.

Luke grunted. "Come on you two, we gotta get going."

They moved slowly down the aisle between the rows of silent, wondering passengers. Behind him Sheriff O'Neill muttered, "If you are Pretty Boy, don't try anything."

THEY STEPPED off the train into the quiet of the Kansas night. The stars were bright overhead and the little group of men stood in a tight knot beside the tracks as the train chugged and puffed and finally gathered itself together enough to move noisely off into the darkness.

Then they were alone. Will felt the limitlessness of the space around him. This was the closest he had gotten to the country itself. He breathed deeply. There was plenty of air for a man to breath, to fill his lungs with. If only Sally hadn't put that germ of doubt in her father's mind everything would have been all right.

The distrust and suspicion in Sheriff O'Neill's eyes bothered and disturbed him. He wouldn't have minded the Billings Gang alone if he had been sure of the Sheriff, but he was no longer sure of him.

It suddenly seemed to Will that he had done a rash and foolhardy thing. The train would get to Wichita sooner than they would. Suppose Sally gave the alarm and a posse came out to meet them, shooting first and asking questions later. Maybe he was as unreliable and stupid as his Uncle was always claiming he was.

The chill night air blew against his cheek, robbing him of his self-confidence. What a fool he had been! It was just like him to try to rush in and help the father and get himself in a mess. Uncle Ephriam couldn't have blamed him too severely if he had lost the eighty thousand dollars in a train robbery.

Through the night Will heard the soft thud of horses' hooves striking the rolling plains. Riding across country all night was going to be far different than riding sedately through the quiet New England countryside. He fingered the little pearl-handled pistol. It was a puny weapon against the .44's the others carried; the medals he had won back home for target practice seemed worthless here where men shot at moving targets and shot to kill.

The horses came up. Rangy, tough little beasts, far different from the well trained pacers he was used to. He swung uneasily into the saddle, aware of Sheriff O'Neill's hostile eyes, and the lurking, shifty eyes of the outlaws.

Will sighed. Paul Revere had taken a little canter from Boston to Lexington and his children and his grandchildren were still talking about it. But nobody would ever talk about Will Dudley's ride across Kansas, or think it anything of a feat. Yet Will was convinced that Revere's ride had been child's play compared to what faced him now.

ONCE IN the saddle his confidence returned. The feel of the

horse between his knees, the reins in his hands brought back that rush of confidence and reckless courage that had possessed him in the train. "Ready?" he shouted.

They rode all night through the darkness, the only sound the pounding of the horses' hooves on the soft ground. There was no talk. They rode grimly, as if they were all aware that somewhere over the next low hill they might meet a posse coming out for them from Wichita or maybe some way-station along the railroad where the alarm had been given.

Will felt the weariness of the long ride stealing over him, numbing his senses. The rhythmic movements of his horse seemed to lull him into a state of semi-consciousness. It was difficult for him to keep alert, yet he realized that his safety depended on his staying awake. The first greyness in the sky behind him was a welcome sight. Perhaps he could stay awake better in the daylight. The dull black shadows they passed in the darkness seemed only rough snatches of poorly remembered dreams. The shape of the tree had passed before he had identified it for what it was.

But daylight brought no surcease from the steady riding. The little band pushed on across the limitless wastes in the blazing sun, they saw no human thing, no sign of human habitation. Each settlement and tiny homestead in this country must be known and avoided by the Billings Gang.

At noon they rested in a tiny gully in the shade of a few cottonwood trees. Will was thirsty and hot; the sun had baked his fair skin lobster red.

Luke Billings watched him with suspicion. Pretty Boy Chauncey would never have burned brick red on the Kansas plains. His skin was tough and used to exposure. Will gulped his steaming coffee trying to hide his cracked hands and blistered face. Cuddled in the palm of his hand was the little pearl-handled pistol. He was careful never to let it out of his hand.

"You burn easy," Luke remarked.

Will raised his head. If he could fight back sleep maybe he would be a match for the big bully. But sleep was ever pulling at his eyelids relaxing his limbs.

"I have a fair skin," he said slowly. "It always burns the first day out." He set down his coffee cup, felt gingerly of his cheek. His beard was beginning to grow again, and judging from the tenderness of his skin, he wouldn't want to shave for days.

His eyes studied Luke's suspicious face. Maybe he'd never shave again.

"I seen tenderfeet burn like that," Luke commented.

"Like I said, I have a tender skin," Will repeated sleepily.

"The air makes 'em sleepy, too," Luke went on slowly.

With an effort Will pushed back the layers of fatigue that rolled over him. "Don't let this trick you into your coffin," he warned as he picked up his coffee cup, felt the warmth of the coffee slide down his parched throat.

Sheriff O'Neill sat across the low fire from him. Will realized uneasily that he should have been beside the lawman. Or had the outlaws purposely separated them? It was hard to stay alert to everything when he was so sleepy.

Luke's voice became soft and silky, strange and unnatural in the bully's mouth. "How about a little cat-nap?" he suggested.

Will Dudley did not move or change a muscle, but the silkiness of Luke's voice had snapped him awake. "Sure," he muttered. Something very strange had happened to Dudley; he had been acting the part of Pretty Boy Chauncey for so long that something of the outlaw's nature had become part of him.

Every vestige of sleep left him, but he leaned back against the trunk of the cottonwood and closed his eyes to almost imperceptible slits.

HE HEARD Sheriff O'Neill stir restlessly. "I guess I should go over and sit beside Pretty Boy," the lawman said with exaggerated carelessness.

"Stay where you are," Luke spoke through barely opened lips.

Will waited, and while he waited he knew why Pretty Boy used the child-like pearl-handled pistol. It could be cupped and hidden completely in a man's fist; the concealed weapon was trained at Luke Billings' heart.

The outlaw spoke softly to the Sheriff. "That's not Pretty Boy. Whatever the game is, it's up. You might as well tell me who he is."

"As far as I know he's who he claims he is," the Sheriff answered evenly.

"Don't be a fool," Luke snapped. "Pretty Boy wouldn't be asleep now, and he wouldn't be burned that way." He drew his heavy six-shooter. "This is one time I'm shooting first and asking questions later."

The big gun leveled slowly at Will. He watched it without fear. He had no compunction about shooting first; the outlaw was prepared to shoot him in cold blood while he slept. After Luke had disposed of him, he would undoubtedly turn his gun on the Sheriff.

The tiny pistol in Will's hand spat fire. A look of bewilderment settled over Luke Billings' face, then he pitched slowly forward on his face.

Instantly Will and the sheriff were on their feet, guns exposed at last. The rest of the Gang were stunned by the suddenness of the attack; they had expected no such outcome to their leader's plans. There was nothing but blank incredulity of their faces as they stared at their fallen chief.

Sheriff O'Neill shrugged as he disarmed them one by one and strapped their hands behind their backs. "These fellows," he commented wryly, "are only heroes when they have control of the business end of a gun."

(Continued On Page 90)

COMING NEXT ISSUE

A *Powerful Complete New Book Length Novel*

by LEE FLOREN

(Author of "Hangman's Range")

Watch For

THIS GUN CAN KILL

in

COMPLETE COWBOY NOVEL MAGAZINE

The big June issue goes on sale April 1st

Johnny Joe Delivers

by BEN FRANK

Johnny Joe knew that lawman Sid Cross was square; he'd get after the cattlemen's ruthless attacks upon their small neighbors; but this would take time, and the little men might be killed off or driven away first . . .

OLD JOHNNY Joe, the peddler, didn't reckon he'd sell much on this trip through the Upper Flats country. What he'd heard back in Flatsburg about the rising trouble between the big and little cattlemen had warned him not to expect much business. When people are riled up and scared and not sure how long they'll be able to hang on to their homes, they just aren't much interested in pins, needles, thread, shoe-laces and such.

But Johnny Joe was on his way. For thirty years, he'd been making the rounds of the scattered nester homes in the Upper Flats country, and he reckoned it'd take more than threats of a range war to stop him this year. Besides, he'd been hearing about this trouble for years, and nothing had ever come of it.

He pulled his old saddle horse to a stop in front of Jim Blue's log ranch house and sat staring at it, his keen blue eyes wide, his thin fingers clutching the saddle horn. The place was deserted; he could see that from

where he sat. It looked like Jim Blue had left so quick he'd forgotten to shut one window and the door and the door kept banging away in the north breeze.

Old Johnny Joe slid stiffly to the ground, hobbled around his pack mule and went into the house. All signs said the Blues had left in a hurry and they'd travelled light. Old Johnny shut the window and door and went back to his horse. A frown pulled at his wrinkled face, and his blue eyes had lost all their usual sparkle.

"Ain't like a man to pull his stakes like that," he muttered, "unless somethin's got him spooked."

And then he remembered the rumors he'd heard back in Flatsburg. Jim Blue was one of the little cattle men.

Johnny went on, riding ahead of his pack mule, following the trail that led deeper into the Upper Flats country. He didn't hurry. He figured he'd make Tom Placer's home about noon and put on the feed bag with

Tom and his wife. And thinking of Tom's wife, a little nervous woman with deep-set eyes, he remembered the medicine in his pocket that old Doc Horn had asked him to deliver to her.

"Reckon she'll just about be outa this sleepin' powder, Johnny," old Doc had said. "She ain't got no business livin' out there, high strung and all nerves like she is."

Johnny patted the pocket. The envelope of medicine was still there along with the little notebook in which he kept his record of sales.

But he didn't eat dinner with Tom Placer; what he saw when he reached Tom's place made him forget all about dinner. A wagon stood in front of the two-roomed house, and Tom and his wife were loading up their possessions as fast as they could.

TOM DIDN'T even have time to stop and talk. "I've had my warnin'," he said, dumping a box of bedding into the wagon. "I reckon this time them cattlemen mean business. They're makin' a last try to run us little fellers out; the wife an' me are holin' up in Flatsburg till the sheriff gets them range hogs corralled."

He showed Johnny Joe the warning note: "*Notice to all cattle rustlers: If you haven't cleared out by sundown, you will have to suffer the consequences. This means you, Tom Placer! A. A.*"

"What's the A-A stand for?" Johnny asked.

"Anti-rustlers Association," Tom said bitterly. "The big cattle men've organized under the name, an' they've branded all us little fellers an' the nesters rustlers. They've chipped in a wad of money an' have hired a bunch of out of state gunmen to do their dirty work for 'em."

Tom's wife climbed up on the old wagon seat. She was crying silently, the tears sliding down her thin cheeks.

Johnny Joe was suddenly angry. He new for sure now why Jim Blue's cabin stood empty. He balled his skinny fists and stuck out his lower lip.

"Them fellers can't do this!" he said between his teeth. "It's worse'n hoss stealin'! What'n tarnation we got a sheriff for? What's the matter with Sid Cross? Why ain't he out here, doin' somethin' to protect yuh boys?"

"Sid's all right," Tom said. "He ain't got no more use for them range hogs than the rest of us. It's just that this trouble has come to a head mighty q u i c k. The A-A's got the jump on Sid, an' right now the A-A's top ramrod. Sid'll be able to do somethin' as soon as he gets organized. Once they're stopped, they won't try it again, I reckon. If us little fellers get to vote at the next election, I reckon we can stop 'em for good."

Tom climbed up beside his wife, slapped the lines over his team and turned toward the trail. "Johnny," he called back over his shoulder. "if I was yuh, I'd high-tail it outa here. Them hired killers might mistake yuh for one of us."

Johnny Joe climbed back into his saddle. He noticed for the first time a chill creeping into the north breeze. It had the smell of blizzard in it, and clouds were stacking up in the north.

He'd forgotten his hunger. His eyes followed Tom's creaking wagon until it was lost below a brush covered rise. Johnny Joe was a fair-minded man, and he knew what this cutting up of the big ranges by the small cattlemen and nesters meant to the big ranches. But knowing that the big ranchers had brought in a pack of hired killers to spook the little fellows out of their hard-won homes before the next election, made his blood boil. It was big money against law and right, and it looked like big money was sitting on top. And if big money got their men elected to office, law and right was in for a set-back. Of course, if the little fellows could hang on until after election, they'd be a different story.

He wasn't worried about himself. Anybody could take one look at him and his outfit and see that he wasn't a nester. But he knew for sure he wasn't going to do any business in the Flats Country. Most likely all the families would be spooked out just like Jim Blue and Tom Placer had been.

HE THOUGHT then of Nate and Martha and the baby, and his heart pounded up in Johnny Joe's throat. Nate wasn't the spooky kind. And neither was Martha—unless she'd be afraid for her baby. Nate would stick to his home; he'd wham away with his old 30-30 until there wasn't any fight left in him.

But on second thought, old Johnny Joe reckoned Nate was probably safe from the cattlemen. Nate had worked for some of the big outfits and had a lot of friends still working for them. Then, Nate's place was in sort of a back woodsy place off the main trail. Besides, Nate had gone in for wheat raising; everybody knew that. He likely didn't have more than one or two old milk cows on the place. The cattlemen wouldn't be worrying about Nate cutting into their herds and they surely wouldn't begrudge him the few acres of ground he'd plowed up.

So when Johnny Joe came to the cut-off to Nate's place, he'd lost all his fear for Nate, Martha and the baby. If he hadn't wanted to see them he'd have gone straight on through the Upper Flats country. But he couldn't pass up Martha. He'd known her ever since she'd cut her first tooth. He'd watched her grow up into a mighty pretty woman and had seen young Nate Nichols fall in love with her. He'd gone to the wedding, and later, played the fiddle for the wedding dance. And the baby—he was a fine baby, and Nate and Martha had named him Johnny Joe! Of course, old Johnny Joe couldn't pass them up.

He swung his horse and mule into the cut-off, and his eyes went to the sky in the north. The blizzard clouds were working closer.

Martha Nichols stood in the doorway of her cabin, the sun gleaming on her golden hair, a smile on her soft, red lips. She was glad to see old Johnny Joe, and invited him in.

He took along his pack, knowing even if Martha didn't have much money to spend, she'd get a buzz out of looking things over. All women were alike that way.

Nate wasn't around. He'd gone to the other side of his place to patch up some fence. At first, little Johnny Joe was half-scared of the old peddler, but he got over that when the old man gave him some peppermints.

Martha let out little cries of delight over some of the things she found in the pack. She had a lot of fun fingering over the bright ribbons and silky scarfs. There was no worry or strain here in this neat little cabin, so Johnny Joe knew that Nate hadn't been warned to get out. He was mighty glad of that, for Nate would likely get his fool self shot before he'd leave his home and his land.

Martha bought a package of needles and some thread, and when old Johnny saw her looking longingly at a bolt of lace, he snipped off a couple of yards and gave it to her. She was as happy as a kid with a new toy.

Old Johnny Joe pulled out his record book to jot down the things Martha had bought, and there was Mrs. Placer's medicine, which he'd forgotten about in the excitement. He put it pack into his pocket, thinking that by now she'd be in Flatsburg where she could get all the medicine she needed.

Martha wanted him to stay the rest of the afternoon and that night, but he said he had to go on, even if he hadn't seen Nate. He wanted to beat the blizzard to Indian Pass. If the pass were closed, he might be tied up in the Upper Flats country for a month. He loaded his pack on the mule, climbed on his horse and rode around Nate's new log barn and past the round pole corral.

SOMETHING white, flapping on the corral gate, caught his eye, and he stopped. It was a piece of paper pinned there with a nail. He glanced back. The barn stood between him and the house. He slid to the ground and looked at the paper. His heart did a flip-flop, and his middle felt like someone was rubbing a piece of ice over it. The paper had some words written on it, and they said. *"Notice to all cattle rustlers: If you haven't cleared out by sundown, you will have to suffer the consequences This means you, Nate Nichols! (Signed) A.A."*

The paper slipped from old Johnny Joe's numb fingers and went scooting off across the field. The wind pressed around him, and the sun went under a cloud. He shivered. A single flake of snow touched his nose and turned into a drop of water.

So Nate was on the Cattlemen's list, after all! And Nate wouldn't run. Johnny Joe knew that. Nate would stay and fight, and he wouldn't have a Chinaman's chance.

Johnny Joe drew a deep breath. He didn't make much difference to anyone whether he lived or died. With Nate it was different. He was young and he had a wife and a child. Nate had to keep on living.

Johnny Joe turned back. Maybe he could help Nate, maybe not. But he would try, even if it cost him his life. He led his horse and mule into the barn and bedded them down for the night. Then he went to the house.

"Changed my mind," he told Martha, "seein' as how it's beginnin' to spit some snow."

Martha was delighted. It wasn't every day that she and Nate had company.

A little later, Nate came, and he just about broke old Johnny's arm, shaking it. "You ol' scoundrel, comin' to see my wife when I ain't at home, eh?" Nate's big mouth wore a wide grin. "Just for that you can get your scissors an' give me a hair cut in the mornin'." He rubbed his stubbly chin. "An', maybe, you can do somethin' with that ol' razor of mine. I think Martha's been usin' it to peel spuds."

While Martha cooked supper, John-sharpened Nate's razor. By the time supper was over, snow was swishing steadily against the window.

"Regular ol'-fashioned b l i z z a r d comin'," Nate said.

Johnny Joe nodded. He felt good about it, too. He reckoned that a bunch of hired gunmen wouldn't be too keen about getting out on a night like this. By tomorrow night, Sid Cross, the sheriff, would likely be doing something about this sudden anti-rustler association business.

Nate fired up the rusty pot-bellied stove until it was a cherry red. "Where's that ol' fiddle of yours?" he asked. "Reckon you wouldn't come without it?"

JOHNNY JOE went out to the barn where he'd left the fiddle with his pack. It was gettting colder all the time, and the snow eddied around like fine sand, turning the ground white in spots. A bad night for riders. Johnny whistled a little tune as he trudged back to the house. In the doorway, he glanced at the barn. It was getting pretty dark, and with the snow, the barn was just a black shape.

He sat down on the chair by the stove, got out the old f i d d l e and tuned it up. Nate doubled his long legs and crouched on the floor with his back to the wall. Martha sat down on the other chair, cradling little Johnny Joe in her arms, her round chin just above Little Johnny's fuzzy yellow hair. Outside, the w i n d howled. Inside, the stove burned merrily, and the smoke curled up lazily from Nate's quirley. Everything was just about perfect. Everything except a little gnawing uneasiness in old Johnny Joe's mind.

He tucked the fiddle under his chin. It felt cold from being out there in the barn. He drew the bow across the strings. The tones came, warm and sweet. He cut right into *"Home on the Range"* and forgot everything except the way Nate sat there, listening, letting his cigarette burn clear up to his fingers. And the way Martha's blue eyes misted over.

Right in the middle of the tune came the knock. It was on the plank door and sounded more like a pistol shot than a knock. It made the door rattle, and it made the blood in old Johnny Joe's thin body run cold. The old fiddle choked off, and the hot stove sighed unhappily.

Before Nate could get his long legs

untangled, Johnny had leaped to his feet and shoved the fiddle into Nate's big hands. "Hold this," he said. "That's likely some lost pilgrim. I'll see."

It's hard for a man to get up from the floor with his hands full of fiddle. Nate sank back to the floor. Martha cuddled the baby up close and rubbed her smooth chin over his fuzzy head. The baby gurgled happily. Old Johnny Joe went to the door, his boots clicking against the bare floor. It was about seven feet from his chair to the door. Seven feet! It seemed more like seven miles.

He got hold of the latch and lifted it. The door opened toward Martha and Nate. They wouldn't be able to see out. That was the way he wanted it, so they couldn't see out and wouldn't be seen from the outside.

He didn't look back, didn't hesitate. He opened the door quickly and stepped outside. Enough light from the door sifted through the fine snow for him to see five riders with shotguns in the crooks of their arms. He pulled the door shut and stood waiting, the snow sifting into his thin hair.

"You Nate Nichols?" a voice rasped.

Old Johnny Joe knew this was likely it. The time for him to die. The moment he told them he was Nate, they'd probably blast him wide open. Then they'd go racing away, not knowing they'd killed the wrong man until after Sheriff Cross had got into action. Then it would be too late for them to do anything about their mistake, and Nate would keep on living.

"Yeah," he said. "I'm Nate Nichols."

He braced himself a little. He felt the muscles across his middle knot up. He waited, but the guns didn't blast.

"Come with us," the voice said.

The riders circled him and cut him away from the house. They led him past the barn and toward the south. He didn't have on his hat or coat. Shivers ran through him.

"Where yuh takin' me?" he chat-tered. "What're yuh goin' to do with me?"

"You had your warnin', Nichols," the leader said, "an' you didn't get out. We're takin' you to the main trail where we'll string you up for the rest of your kind to see!"

Johnny Joe had figured on a quick death. No pain. No strangling. Just a sharp, white blasting of the life from his old body. But now—

He stumbled and went to his knees. A rider swore, reached down and jerked him to his feet.

"Reckon this here hombre's legs is givin' out," the man drawled, and the others laughed.

They plodded on, the wind at their backs. They came to the main trail and followed it into a little hollow. They stopped under a scraggly cottonwood, and someone lit a lantern. The men slid down from the saddles.

JOHNNY JOE saw them then, all strangers, and about the toughest looking outfit he'd ever run up against. One of the men had a jug fastened to his saddle. He took a swig and passed it around to the others. Then he lifted the lantern and squinted at Johnny Joe's face.

"Hell, Mac," he said, "I thought this Nate Nichols was a youngish jasper."

The leader of the gang came over. His blocky face wore a frown.

"You Nate Nichols?" he asked again.

"Yeah," Johnny Joe husked. "Who do yuh think I am—Santa Claus?"

"Don't be funny," Mac said. "Yo're in for trouble!"

Johnny Joe shivered, and it wasn't altogether from the biting cold. "Yuh skunks're in fer a peck of trouble yourselves," he gritted.

One of the men said, "Hell, Mac, what're we waitin' for?"

Another man shinned up the cottonwood and looped a rope over a limb. "How's this for length?" he asked.

A man led a horse under the rope. "About right, I'd say," was the answer.

Johnny Joe eyed that swinging rope. It turned him sick. He'd seen .

a man hung once; the man had died slowly with his feet churning the empty air.

Mac turned Johnny toward the light. "You wouldn't be just tellin' us yo're Nichols, would you?"

Johnny Joe suddenly felt scared. Some for himself, but mostly for Nate and Martha and the baby back there in the cabin. He had to make these men believe they were hanging the right man.

He doubled his right fist. It wasn't a very big fist. "Of course, I'm Nichols, yuh murderin' shunk!" he yelled, and flung the fist at the man's nose.

The fist never landed. Mac simply ducked back, and that was all there was to it. "Search him," Mac ordered quietly.

The men grabbed Johnny, and hopelessness swamped him. He remembered the record book in his pocket. That would be a dead giveaway. Sure enough, the men found the book right off and gave it to the leader.

Mac thumbed through the little book. He found Johnny's name and business and address in the back of it. He laughed, but there wasn't any fun in it. He took hold of Johnny's shirt front and twisted it up under Johnny's chin until the oldster could scarcely breathe. "So yo're Nate Nichols!" he grated. "Like hell!"

He gave Johnny a shove, and the oldster went down in a heap on the snowy ground.

"For some reason," Mac said, "this ol' fool has misled us, boys. He's not Nate Nichols. Nichols is a younger man. Likely he was scared crazy—or he's pulled a fast one on us!"

The men milled around Johnny Joe, cursing angrily.

"The rope's waitin'," someone said. "Let's hang him!"

"Hold your hosses, boys," Mac said. "We're paid to clean out certain people, and I reckon there ain't no Johnny Joe on our list; we ain't hangin' people for the fun of it."

HE TURNED to Johnny Joe and flung the little record book at him.

"If you wasn't an ol' man," he grated, "I'd beat the livin' daylights outa you just for the hell of it! As it is I reckon you can go. But if you cross our trails again, we'll turn your hide into a sieve. An' if yo're bright yo'll forget what happened tonight!"

Johnny Joe gathered up the notebook. His fingers were so cold and shaky that he could hardly do anything with them. His teeth clicked like seeds in a dried gord, and he reckoned he was the coldest he'd ever been in his life. He eyed the whisky jug longingly. "I'm a-freezin'," he shivered. "I could use a shot o' that liquor."

"Give him a drink," Mac said, "We'll all have a good snort. By now Nichols'll probably be wised up to what's goin' on. We may need a little bracin' to help us smoke him out."

A man held out the jug.

"We ought put a rope around his neck instead of good liquor down it," he growled.

Johnny Joe took the jug eagerly. He tipped it against his blue lips and took a swallow. The stuff was liquid fire. He could feel it all the way down. It sent little needles of warmth through him. It was just what he needed. He hovered over the jug like he would over a warm stove, hugging it to him, hating to give it up.

A man reached for the jug, but Johnny Joe wasn't ready to give it up. He backed into the shadows. He lifted it for another swig, but he never got it.

The man jerked a jug away from him. "Don't drink it all, you ol' devil!" he said.

The man drank and passed the jug to the next man, who drank and passed it on. The leader was the last to drink. He wiped his hand across his lips and shoved the cork firmly into the jug.

"Now," he said, glaring at Johnny Joe, "to go back after Nate Nichols!"

The men swung into their saddles. One of the men looked back at Johnny Joe. He lifted his shotgun until it was level with the oldster's middle. He laughed harshly, lowered the gun and followed his companions.

JOHNNY JOE let the air out of his lungs in a relieved "pooh." He felt as weak as a day-old calf. And sick—sick because he hadn't fooled these men. Sick because Nate was on their death list, and they were headed back after him. But Johnny knew he'd done all he could to help Nate. And a man can do no more than his best.

He stumbled to his feet and turned back toward Nate's little home. The snow peppered against his face and clung to his eyebrows. The wind cut like whips. He beat his hands together, trying to get the blood back into them. And all the time, he listened for shots to come drifting on that icy north wind.

But no shots came. He stumbled on, fighting the wind and snow. He figured, maybe, the killers had decided to wait until morning to get Nate. If they had, he might be able to slip back and help him. Or maybe, just maybe, his little trick had worked, and the riders wouldn't get to Nate's place at all. He hoped that was the way it was, but he wouldn't count too much on that.

It was a long way back. He'd begun to think the wind had shifted and he'd gotten off the trail, when he heard horses in the underbrush. He turned toward the sound and went sliding down into a little gully. He saw the horses before he saw the men. He moved cautiously through the brush toward the place where the men had bedded down for the night in the lee of a bluff.

He approached noiselessly on hands and knees, but the horses caught his scent and snorted a little. He could see the five men now, dark shadows on the ground, all bunched up like a herd of cold yearlings. They were sleeping. And they kept right on sleeping. He could hear them snore now that he was out of the wind.

Johnny Joe sneaked one of the horses away, climbed into the saddle and went tearing toward Nate's cabin. It wasn't so very far, and the light shining out from the window was about the most welcome sight he'd ever seen. He was pretty careful how

he went up to the door, for Nate, he reckoned, knew by now that something was up, and he'd likely be in there with the old 30-30 in his hands.

Before he got too close to the door, he called, "Nate, it's me, Johnny Joe!"

The door flew open. "Come in," Nate said in a tight voice.

Johnny went in. Sure enough, Nate stood there with the rifle.

"What's up, Johnny?" he whispered. "Is it the cattlemen? Is somebody settin' a trap for me?"

Johnny shut the door against the cold. He made a bee-line for the stove. Martha poked her head out from the back room, her eyes wide with fright. Johnny gave her a reassuring grin and held his thin hands over the stove. That heat sure felt good.

"There's a trap, Nate," he said, "but she's sprung. The Anti-rustlers Association's hired killers come to get yuh tonight, goin' to make sure yuh didn't vote. But they mistook me fer yuh; when they learned their mistake, they turned me loose. They started back fer yuh, but stopped out of the wind in a gully to get a little shut-eye. Soon's I get some of this heat soaked up, yuh an' me'll take us some ropes an' go tie 'em up. I reckon Sheriff Cross'll kinda be happy to get his hands on 'em. With 'em put where they belong in jail, I reckon there won't be no more trouble, 'for yuh little fellers'll carry the election two to one."

"But, Johnny," Nate gulped, trying to keep up with what Johnny Joe was telling him, and having trouble doing it, "them fellers may wake up before we get there an'—"

"Nope," Johnny Joe said. "I reckon they won't—not for along time, they won't."

He pulled the empty medicine envelope out of his pocket.

"Yuh see," he went on grinning, "I poured Mrs. Placer's sleepin' powder in them skunks' whiskey jug! Why, thunderation, Nate, I reckon them boys won't wake up 'fore noon tomorrow."

Dismukes grappled with the lawmen as the rock fell.

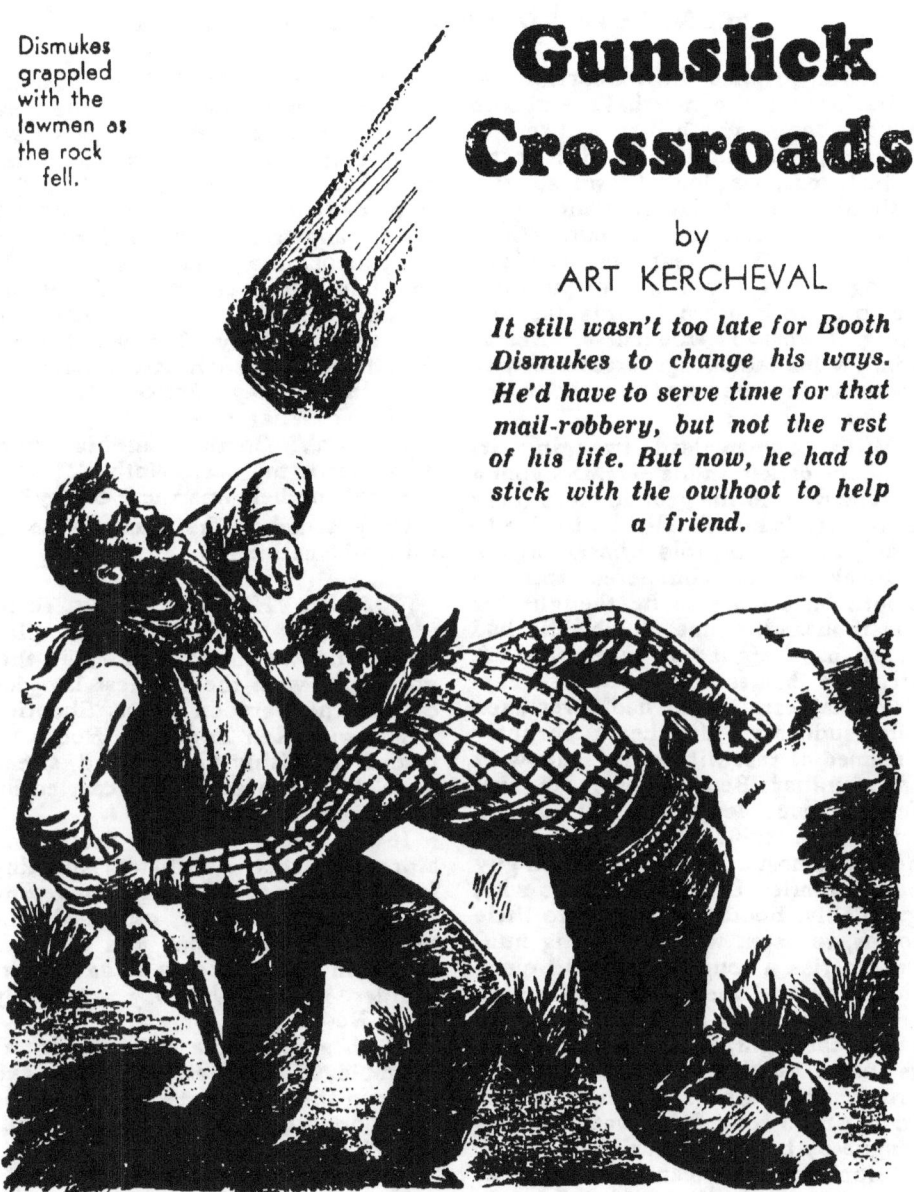

Gunslick Crossroads

by
ART KERCHEVAL

It still wasn't too late for Booth Dismukes to change his ways. He'd have to serve time for that mail-robbery, but not the rest of his life. But now, he had to stick with the owlhoot to help a friend.

BOOTH Dismukes allowed that neither a U.S. Marshal nor a rival outlaw was going to stop him from reaching Smiley Larkin. Smiley was in a bad way and needed Booth's help; Larkin would get help, no matter how much deeper Booth had to sink himself into this black mess of his own mixing.

Big-shouldered, rawboned Booth holed up in this dank cave in the as- pen-yellowed Benediction Mountains, felt his bucking six-guns grow hot against the fading chill of dawn. He dreaded to kill a lawman, so he kept placing his lead just short of every bob of hat and flash of Coltbarrel down the slope; Dismukes wanted only to halt Ken Rockman, the age- less, lean-jowled marshal who had trailed him from the mail-car stickup on Kinnikinnick Pass.

Booth grinned in humorless admiration for the marshal's stubborn pluck. Booth, who had turned to outlawry for the sheer hell of it, after a torturous, war-long dream about a pair of laughing blue eyes and generous red lips had turned sour. Who'd chalked up two years of headlong plunges into adventure, of heedless gambles with death in this fast-settling Colorado wilderness. Beside him lay his saddlebags, crammed with loot—money that would give Smiley Larkin a chance.

With lawman lead twanging its ominous offkey in his ears, the young outlaw hugged the ground close there at the cave's mouth. He had to live to reach Smiley, he told himself again.

Bleak horror shuddered through Booth once more as he thought for the thousandth time of what he had heard on a night two weeks ago. A siege of homesickness, new to his devil-may-care soul, had overtaken him suddenly. His heart abruptly dreamed of rest within the shadow of the familiar Benedictions. He suffered an acute longing to fill his eyes with home sights, to hear voices that he knew, most of all to see a swell guy named Smiley Larkin. That was why, guardedly, Booth had gone into little towns, to listen with increasing hunger, to risk a couple of careful questions now and then before riding on.

In a saloon up at Steerhide, Colorado, that night, he'd keened his ears as usual toward jumbles of half-drunken talk. And Booth had further l o o s e n e d one mellowed fellow's tongue by buying the drinks.

"Lupine?" The man had stared at him. "You headin' for Lupine, stranger? T'other side of the mountains. Can't miss it—"

"Ain't never been thre," Booth cut in casually. "How's things down there?"

"Right thrivin', Mister. R i g h t thrivin'. Bad fire, though, a few nights back. Burned down the blind saddlemaker's place.

Cold washed through Booth's veins; half-formed realization bolted him up stiff, almost jolting the glass from his hand. "Blind—saddlemaker? Blind?"

The other nodded. "Best damned saddlemaker in the state. Fella name o' Smiley Larkin. Blinded two years ago, they say, helpin' some outlaw gent that was a friend of his. Gun exploded in his face. The fire? Old Man Sandstrom, runs a feed store next door, too danged skinflint to put hay under cover. Stacks it any place. Hay caught fire and burnt down the saddlery. Dammed shame it didn't burn old Sandstrom with it!"

"Blind. Smiley. *Oh, Gawd....*"

"Huh? What you say?"

"Nothin'." Booth spun his empty glass down the bar. "Nothin'."

What the hell was there to say?

Only somehow he must do something—something—

WELL, HE was doing something, Booth reflected, flat-lipped; he was shooting it out in thin gray light with the canniest law dog east of the Paradox River. Shooting it out with Ken Rockman. Booth reloaded feverishly and slipped, silent, from the cave's mouth. He carried his crammed saddlebags.

It was a case of life or death now. More than that. Booth was shooting for a chance to take this money to Smiley Larkin. He glimpsed the shadowed wraith that was Marshal Rockman making for a huge granite boulder. Working his way inexorably up to Booth.

Booth grabbed the slim moment to scramble to his feet, half skid and half run the short distance downslope to the opposite side of the same boulder. There was a long silence of deadly waiting.

The mail train had yielded a golden harvest to Booth's guns. A golden harvest, reposing there in Booth's saddlebags, marked by Booth for Smiley Larkin. Booth would get that wealth to Smiley, too. All hell and Kayson Quay wouldn't stop him!

Black-h a t t e d, sandy-mustached, chill-eyed Kayson Quay was fast becoming a hated and feared Western legend, yet terrifyingly real. Memory of Quay brought cold, bracing challenge to Booth. Ace of all killing

(Continued On Page 88)

A Brand New Book

Length Novel

by CLARENCE MULLEN

BULLETS

FOR BALLOTS

At first I didn't see it. There were the braided scatter rugs, the golden maple furniture with the orange plaid cushions and the old-fashioned fireplace still piled high with birch logs. Everything in its place, just as it had been on my previous visit. And then I heard the noise again—muffled, gurgling, like somebody trying to talk and choking over the words. It came from somewhere near the fireplace.

I found her sprawled on her haunches in front of the sofa, her right cheek buried in the plaid cushion, her ebony hair fanned out in thick waves around her face. A bloody bubble had formed on her lips and it burst as she tried to mumble something to me.

I bent over her. "Donna," I cried, "What happened, baby?"

When she didn't answer, I slipped my hand under her cheek and raised her head, ever so gently. Her coal-black eyes opened and for an instant, a sickly smile crossed her face as she recognized me. Then she gave a convulsive shudder, her eyes got glassy and she went limp. Gently laying her head back on the blood-stained sofa, I peered down at her. There was a blood-soaked patch on her white satin blouse where a knife had pierced it. Her own hand was still gripping the handle of the knife.

She had died while I knelt there watching. Strangely, I felt sorry for her—this vampire who had tried to slip me a mickey, or just possibly a bindle of heroin or morphine. And then again, remembering Leila Ames, it suddenly dawned on me that my ace in the hole had been trumped by death!

Complete In The Big March Issue of

CRACK

DETECTIVE

STORIES

COMPLETE COWBOY NOVEL MAGAZINE

(Continued From Page 86)

badmen, Quay had cut his wild rep
in half a dozen states, including a
smoky stay in the Hole-in-the-Wall
country. Wherever the huge outlaw
chose to tarry, that place he claimed
as his own for as long as he cared to
remain. Just now he'd put his defiant brand on the Benedictions and
the towns around. Kayson Quay, with
the fabulous price on his head—

"Come in with me, Dismukes," he'd
recently invited Booth. "I like your
nerve, and I'll make it worth your
while. Gent with your gunspeed is
just wastin' his talents on penny-ante
stuff. There's a mail train comin'
through here...."

"Not a chance," Booth had refused.
"I take orders from nobody, and I
follow my own style; don't bother
Uncle Sam."

Then he'd learned about Smiley,
and an agony of self-blame had
driven Booth forth, single-handed, in
the black drizzle of night before last,
to train his guns on the railway mail.
Double-crossing Kayson Quay by
pulling the job ten miles farther
north! Booth's biggest haul—and he
would dump every cent of it in
Smiley's lap. His wild, awkward way
of making amends. Lawman Rockman nor Outlaw Quay nor anybody
was going to stand between him and
his plans!

But Rockman had tried. Hounded
him with relentless coldness through
twenty-four hours of ceaseless, lead-
filled hide and seek. Only a few feet
from him, now, Rockman's voice
rang sharply: "This is the end for
you, Dismukes! Toss your gun out
where I can see it!"

"I got just as much chance as
you, Rockman," Booth hurled at him.

On a sudden inspiration Booth
dropped his saddlebags to pick up
a small boulder with his left hand.
For an instant his eyes swept the
curve of the rock some six feet above
him. And then his well-aimed missile
sailed upward, caromed off the slop-
ing granite, came bounding down beyond Booth's vision.

As he'd hoped, the ricochet evidently put the marshal in started expect-
ancy of a bashed-in skull. The man
sprang wide of the falling boulder.

GUNSLICK CROSSROADS

And Booth had him. He crashed his big frame into Rockman, left hand seizing that gun wrist, twisting it violently until the marshal's powerless fingers released the weapon. Booth still carried one gun, and he jammed the barrel into the lean midriff before him, staggering the lawman backwards.

"That's it, sit down!" Booth snapped. "It's easier to take off your boots that way."

"Huh?" The man looked up quizzically.

BOOTH put a deadly crackle into his voice then and Rockman hastened to obey him. Rockman's boots came off easily to his tugs; he flung them at Booth's feet.

"I'll leave you your socks," Booth said, grabbing up the boots but still keeping his Colt readied on the lawman. "This country's rough on bare feet."

Rockman ventured to full height. "Have your little joke, Dismukes. Some day—"

"What I'm doin'," Booth said bitterly, "is no joke!"

"Damned if you ain't a sticker in my craw, Dismukes!" Rockman shook his head. "Most your jobs not raisin' too much stink up till now—liftin' a roll off a tinhorn gambler, or runnin' off beeves now and then from syndicate ranches. Like maybe you was only huntin' excitement. Then all at once you grab a punch marked 'U. S. Mail'. Why, Dismukes?"

"You figure it out, tin badge," Booth rumbled testily. "Me, I'm too busy."

"You won't always win," Rockman pointed out.

(Continued On Page 90)

Another Top-Notch
Book-Length Novel

The Stranger From Texas

by Allan K. Echols
is in the April issue of
Blue Ribbon Western

A NEW NOVELETTE

By a Famous Author

ELI COLTER

Boothill Waits For Sundown

Appears Complete in April
FAMOUS WESTERN on Sale Feb. 1.

NOVEL MAGAZINE COMPLETE COWBOY

(Continued From Page 89)

"I'll play till I lose, then," Booth clipped.

"There's a crossroads for every man. You took the wrong fork, and went too far, when you started tamperin' with Uncle Sam."

Booth snorted, an hour later, at memory of the omen in Rockman's voice. After all, he had the marshal's horse, his gun, and his boots. He had the loot. He was riding his big black and leading the lawman's prancy buckskin.

He stopped at a creek to water the horses. He could have told Rockman a lot of things. About a tough-hided little yonker who grew up to become eventually Booth Dismukes, the bad one. From a scrawny start in life in his pa's creaky sawmill, to the flashier existence of a cowpuncher—and finally to war on a hill called San Juan, under the command of a great rough-ridin' soldier named Teddy. Fighting to come back to the living reality of a dream. Marilee Blakiston of the laughing eyes and eager lips, Marilee, who sang in the *Golden Heart*. Her whispered promise to wait. Coming back to have the dream explode in his face. To view the cheapness and callousness of her as she flung his unwanted ring at him and ran off with the coffee salesman.

He crushed the life out of his cigarette, bleakly musing. The night she and her coffee man had left Lupine, he'd oiled his old sixshooter, packed his warbag, cast about for a first gesture of defiance against the world. Every kid in Lupine had always hated penny-pinching Old Man Sandstrom. Booth tried to talk Smiley into joining him. Smiley, who'd gone to school with him, worked the same trout pools with him. Who'd served in Cuba in the same outfit, and who'd gone back to his trade of making saddles in his little shop in Lupine. Smiley had refused in his blunt, clean-cut, honest way, looking at Booth like he was loco. So Booth went alone that night and robbed Old Man Sandstrom. The loot was twenty-five dollars and thirty-four cents.

BOOTH'S lips clamped tight, and the ugly past stayed with him like a searing burn. After pulling that first job, with his roused home town on his heels, he'd ridden with death only a span away. Riden desperately into the Benedictions. To find, of a sudden, Smiley Larkin sitting a fast saddle alongside. To find Smiley shouting in his ear, "I reckon I got to do this much for you, Booth. But I'm aimin' to stay clean with the law." Smiley'd jerked out a plan and put it into effect before Booth could protest.

He'd lured the posse away from Booth with high-shooting guns, given Booth his chance to ride through a gap in the closing circle of men—to freedom! And Booth had found out only two weeks ago in Steerhide. Those decoy shots.... A defective gun exploding in Smiley's face.... The light blasted from Smiley's eyes.

Crossroads, the marshal had said. Yes, that had been a crossroads. He'd gone down the wrong fork. Smiley—

After two years, Booth was riding back. Back to do what he could for Smiley. Booth shied off the main going as he reached the foothills of the Benedictions. He kept to the cover of brush and rocks with his usual outlaw vigilance. It was full dark when he sat his horse on a hill and looked down at the lights of Lupine. A painful swell of loneliness knotted his throat at first. Then he left Rockman's horse with reins trailing under a cottonwood and nudged his black warily forward into the sprawling town.

Riding along a familiar alley, taking care his horse's hoofs did not strike a clutter of tincans, Booth was hit by sudden premonition that he'd better get things done fast here. Somehow he felt this was building up to—to another crossroads. Ken Rockman was likely still limping through the Benedictions, but you never could tell. Booth had to be long gone from Lupine when the marshal trailed into the town.

Careful inquiry of a stranger told Booth where Smiley was staying—in an old log shack at the north end of town. By a roundabout way he came to the place. He dismounted,

(Continued On Page 92)

COMPLETE COWBOY NOVEL MAGAZINE

(Continued From Page 91)

flung his saddlebags across his shoulder and went forward, hand wary over his gun. He tried the door, pushed into the lamplit room.

A man puttering at the stove in the back of the room whirled at the sound. A familiar figure straightened, and Smiley looked—that is, Smiley's blank, scarred eyes turned toward him. It hit Booth like a mule's kick in the solar plexus.

"Who is it?" The deep, quiet voice was steady and assured as ever.

Booth couldn't answer. He had never dreamed it would be like this. The pain inside him was a tearing, wrenching thing. He could only stand and gulp for air. Smiley, in the strained silence, stepped swiftly backward to the bed, fisted the pillow.

"Smiley!" Booth's voice was a hollow croak in his own ears. "Smiley, I didn't—" He couldn't go on.

But a grin of amazed joy lit Smiley's face.

"Booth! Booth, you old sidewinder!"

Then somehow they were gripping hands, and there was no need for any words between them.

"What's the matter with your other hand?" He demanded. It was bandaged, and Smiley held it carefully at his side.

SMILEY gave a careless shrug. "Oh, that. It's on the mend. Burned it when the shop went up in smoke."

"My Gawd!" said Booth. Smiley couldn't ply his trade with one hand and no eyes. And it might be a long time—

"Hell of a note," Smiley chuckled. "I go through a war without so much as a sprained ankle, and the minute I get home I start gettin' bunged up every time I turn around."

"All on account of me!" The words tore themselves from Booth.

"Ah, don't talk like that," Smiley rumbled.

"But dammit, Smiley, I didn't know! Didn't know a thing about it till a gent up at Steerhide told me

(Continued On Page 94)

COMPLETE COWBOY NOVEL MAGAZINE

(Continued From Page 92)

two weeks ago. That's what tears me to pieces, Smiley. I feel like it was me pulled the trigger that night. Me that made you like this!"

"Now shut your big trap," Smiley ordered affectionately. "You always were a sentimental stiff."

Booth had the odd feeling that he was the one handicapped, desperate, at a loss. After a little Smiley went on quietly.

"You know, Booth, a fella has a lot of time to think when there's no distractions before his eyes. I've figured out a lot of things, especially about you and me. Oh, I was pretty bitter, at first. But it wasn't your fault. It wasn't anybody's fault, unless maybe mine, for hornin' in on your life. So I made up my mind to learn to get along this way, and I am. I'm a good saddlemaker, Booth."

Abruptly Booth rose and brought the saddlebags to drop at Smiley's feet. "There's enough money in here to tide you over, Smiley, till that hand gets well," he said huskily. "Enough money to set you in the best saddleshop in Colorado!"

Smiley's face abruptly sobered. "What kind of money, Booth?"

There was heavy breathless silence in the room. Booth broke it with, "What difference does that make? Smiley, don't be a fool! You can't—" He stopped as Smiley shook his head.

"It's mail-train loot. We heard all about it around here."

Booth was staggered. This was the last, crushing kickback. Smiley wouldn't accept his offer of help! It had never occurred to Booth that Smiley would refuse. Yet he should have known. Hell, he should have known so many things! His coming here hadn't accomplished a thing.

He stared long at Smiley, conscious of growing pride in his friend. Pride that he had lifted himself above bitterness and helplessness. More of a man than Booth Dismukes could ever hope to be. A blind saddlemaker, about him a smattering of greatness.

Booth's mind filled in the rest of the story now. The posse coming upon Smiley, all shot to hell there on the

GUNSLICK CROSSROADS

trail. The months in the hospital. Then the town of Lupine perhaps winking an eye at justice and sort of neglecting to charge Smiley with aiding and abetting. Smiley adjusting himself to a new life of darkness and, Booth reckoned, making better saddles than ever. Till this latest accident happened!

"Smiley," Booth tried again, "there are times for everything. Now is no time for you to be squeamish about where money comes from. Where I got it is no matter. It's all I can do, and—"

SMILEY said gently, "Why don't you give yourself up, Booth? Serve your time in Canyon City. Get yourself a clean start and come back here. You and me pardners, then, in the saddle business. There's more good than bad in you, Booth. I've never stopped thinkin' so."

So here it was. The crossroads again. He'd sensed it coming, and now he knew he had no time to ponder his choice. Back there along his trail Marshal Rockman was sock-footing his dogged way.

"All right." He answered indirectly too. "You won't take it. But I'm not quittin' town till I figure some way—"

The slamming door sliced off the sentence. Booth spun, hand reaching toward his gun, stopping.

Kayson Quay, his Colt level, strode toward them!

Booth, instantly the death-gambler again, stood waiting. His eyes darted searchingly around, calculating everything in the shred of a second. He saw Smiley sit down on the bed.

The black-hatted, sandy-mustached killer spoke. "Somebody shoulda told you, Dismukes. Young 'uns don't double-cross Kayson Quay!"

Booth grinned bleakly. "This young 'un did, Quay." Sensing the sheer love of murder in the huge bandit, he thought. *My mistake. This is the real crossroads, now. For me and Smiley, both.*

Quay intoned, "You shoulda known you couldn't do it and live!"

No use waiting for it. Booth rushed

(Continued On Page 98)

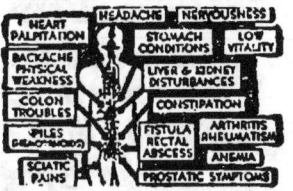

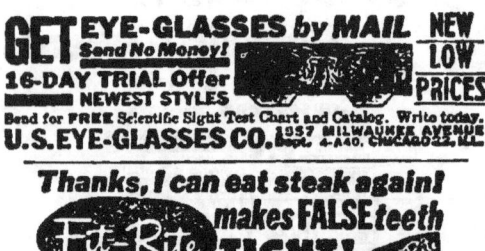

(Continued From Page 77)

Will Dudley had gotten his second wind. He was no longer tired or sleepy. He liked the look of the hot plains, liked the respect in the Sheriff's eyes. No one in Boston had ever looked at him like that; he rather thought after the business for his Uncle was finished he might take his commission and settle down in Wichita.

"There'll be a posse coming out to meet us," Sheriff O'Neill went on, "and maybe we can find some bacon grease in one of these saddle bags to rub on your hands and face. You sure look awful."

"My thin skin came near costing me my life," Will grinned.

The Sheriff regarded him soberly. "It was a good stunt. I knew the game was up when I saw you beginning to burn. When you acted like you were falling asleep, I thought we was both goners."

"It wasn't an act to begin with," Will admitted.

He thought of the Sheriff's pretty blue-eyed daughter and thinking of Sally that Kansas plain seemed even more attractive. "I was thinking much the same thing," he grinned as he mounted his horse.

Sheriff O'Neill prodded the outlaws into the saddle. "Incidentally, there's a reward out for this Billings Gang. I'll split it with you for a stake in these parts."

"My Uncle Ephraim thinks I don't amount to much, but with the right kind of encouragement maybe I could reform," Will picked up the reins, urged his horse forward.

"A man," the Sheriff replied, "is entitled to his opinion, but from what I've seen, I could give your Uncle an argument; maybe you just didn't fit in back East."

* * *

They met the posse about two hours later, and to his surprise Will saw Sally was with them. It was something to see the worry and concern fade from her eyes, see the happiness flooding into her face as she

PRETTY BOY

grew aware of the situation. Then expectedly she began to laugh; there was no hint of hysteria in her laughter, it was just pure merriment.

Will was a little ruffled. It was hardly the welcome he expected her to give him. "You should see your face!" she exclaimed when she had grew aware of the situation. Then unrecovered her breath. "Beet red!" She was off in gales of laughter again.

He urged his horse over to her. "Only way to stop ridicule," he said as he took her in his arms and kissed her. "Right now," he continued in his clipped Boston accents, "you can start paying your husband the proper respect."

Her lips, yielding against his told her answer.

POP ZIMCO—PRINTER

(Continued From Page 68)

Old newspaper files speak eloquently of Pop's ability as a printer and composer of touching obituaries. So far as is known he never killed anyone with that heavy gun, but he could use it expertly? He could cut a fine rope in two at thirty paces; he could knock tin cans spinning hitting them every time, at a reasonable distance.

Pop Zimco was dead when they found him and his type was scattered all around the scene of the tragedy. The wagon contained a hand press and several drawers of different size type. It was a complete layout. On the canvas curtain was the following:

Zimco's Job Printing Shop. Handbills, posters, and newspapers printed. Advertise with Zimco in his Saturday Express.

He was buried near Dodge City when his friends wrote on his tombstone:

His body lies beneath this stone But his soul still lives in Dodge.
Born April 1826
Died July 7, 1894

THE END

(Continued From Page 95)

him. Charged headlong for that death-laden muzzle. But even as his boots racketed on the floor he heard gun thunder. A giant hand slammed him with mountainous force. He careened helplessly.

As he rolled Booth snatched iron reflexively. Another shot blasted out. Then hot lead spurted from his own six.

Kayson Quay crumpled slowly. His gun bucked and roared once even after he was hit. Yet Quay was dead when he struck the floor.

"Booth! Booth, are you all right?"

Booth stared vaguely at Smiley, there on the bed. In Smiley's hand was a gun—probably snatched from beneath the pillow—a ropey blue haze trailing ceilingward from it.

"Sure. I'm okay, Smiley." He gripped his bleeding shoulder. Smiley had shot him! Grasping the fact that death was sweeping into the cabin, Smiley had fired at the first sound he heard, made by Booth's leap toward Quay. No doubt saved Booth's life by knocking him out of Quay's line of fire.

"That's the damnedest thing I ever saw!" he husked, putting the right amount of awe into his voice. "Smiley, you've killed *Kayson Quay!*"

Smiley blinked. "You mean the outlaw?" he demanded .

"Shootin' by sound alone!" Booth went on, as if in unbelief. "Holy smokes! Say! Did you know there's rewards offered for this gent, dead or alive, in half a dozen states? Man, you're rich! You can put up the best saddle shop in the West."

"But cripes!" Smiled was dazed. "It musta been sheer luck—"

"Law comin', Booth," S m i l e y stated, and now Booth's ears too caught the rising crescendo of sound. Attracted by the gun shots, men were running toward the cabin. Smiley was reaching to grip that bleeding shoulder. Booth sidestepped. "Give yourself up, Booth. A few years—and you'll be back here. You and me.... pardners."

Booth laughed recklessly. "Thanks anyway, Smiley. But I got to miss seein' a man. Name of Rockman. I'll take my saddlebags. You won't be needin' 'em."

"No," agreed Smiley.

"Tell Rockman they'll be under that big rock near the pine tree where we used to carve our initials. If he asks why, tell him I said to figure it out himself; I'll be too busy."

HE TURNED back from the door, reached forth a handful of silver and currency. "Twenty-five dollars and thirty-four cents." Money he had never spent. Souvenier of his first job. "Buy Rockman a pair of boots with it, compliments of Old Man Sandstrom. Tell him I said good huntin'!"

He bolted out and hit saddle. Men were swarming on the place. Booth rode hard.

Once clear of the town, he stopped briefly to look at his wound, tie his neckerchief around it. He deposited the loot under the big rock, mounted again, and pounded beneath the stars toward the Benedictions. Not until he had toiled up to the beginning of Mammoth Pass did he pull up.

There was a crossroads here. The straight fork led back to Lupine; the crooked one twisted off into the unknown. For a minute he neck-reined his horse around and looked back along that straight fork, out over the darkened valley, half a smile touching his face.

Down there, safe and secure now, was Smiley Larkin. Great old Smiley. Booth could still join him. Serve out some years in Canyon City, or even Leavenworth. He wouldn't be so old when they put up the sign, *Larkin and Dismukes, Saddlemakers.* A pat hand for Booth Dismukes, but how could you get any excitement out of playing a pat hand? When you already held slim cards in a really high-ante game, even if eventually the law's long reach raked in the pistol jackpot!

Booth reined the black around fast to the other Fork. With his old grin, he leaned over the saddle horn and put many crooked miles between himself and the pursuing marshal.

THE END

www.ingramcontent.com/pod-product-compliance
Lightning Source LLC
Chambersburg PA
CBHW08083250626
47160CB00008B/2943